THEY COME
AT
WHAT YOU LOVE

PS Cleary

Bill Quinn's saga continues. Finally, knowing Michelle is his daughter, with his past continuing to haunt him with the ultimate threat against his daughter, continuing to navigate between his past while trying to move forward. In the end, Bill will do whatever it takes to protect the people most important to him.

Table Of Contents

Acknowledgment

They Come at What You Love is the sequel in this trilogy. It was originated with the intent of how Bill would develop a relationship with Michelle, as well as Eva after getting an answer to his question. It also shows what any father would do to protect his daughter.

I'd like to thank Mr. and Mrs. Roberts. They helped in the editing process, offering suggestions, encouragement. They've been instrumental in helping to develop alternatives to what I had initially envisioned.

I like to thank Rob Scheinerman and Suzanne Reyes for their encouragement and review of the material when I asked for it. Their feedback, enthusiasm and support, I'll always be grateful for. They were instrumental in helping me turn this into a trilogy

Lastly, I can't thank my wife enough throughout this time. She's read this material several times, instrumental in helping me develop the timeline, characters, situations in the material. She helped me define many of the character's motivation. We didn't always agree, but she was helpful in keeping me balanced. Her support over this time has been my inspiration.

Foreword
Early November 2024

It was a stormy night in Galveston, with sideways pouring rain—the kind that made it hard to see. Bill waited for the next shoe to drop with Seamus DeValera, seeing him in Austin, then following them out of town.

On the ride back, Bill told Michelle, "Need to call Tommy."

Tommy picked up. "Hey, skipper. How's the UT trip?"

Bill tensely replied, "Listen. Get to my place, saddle up the horses. I've got Michelle with me, so I can't explain it all. We're being followed, pretty sure I know who. Saddle up!"

Tommy replied, "All right, Skipper. Got your six. Who's following you?"

Bill responded, "Owen's brother."

Tommy started talking. "What the hell's that noise?"

Tires screeched, followed by a large BOOM from the ramming of two cars. Fortunately, they only traded paint. Seamus tried to speed up alongside them, veering into their lane, looking irate, attempting to force them off the road.

After trading paint, Tommy yelled, "Skipper, you okay?"

Bill replied, "Affirmative. Michelle, go in the glove box. Hand me the weapon."

Michelle sat in shock, motionless.

Bill yelled, "Get me the damn weapon now!"

Michelle reached into the glove box, grabbed his XDA45 ACP, and handed it to Bill. The magazine was already in the weapon. With his left hand on the wheel, Bill pushed down on the console, pushing the slide down to ensure he had a round in the chamber. Seamus was coming in for another round of bumper cars.

Bill said to Michelle, "Hang on. Put your seat back, lay down, and keep your head covered."

Michelle did what Bill asked without question, as this was for her protection. Tommy was yelling in the background, but Bill needed to focus, as Seamus had come up alongside them. What Seamus didn't see was Bill opened the driver's side window before drawing his weapon. As Seamus pulled up alongside, Bill stuck his weapon out the window, shooting out his right front tire. After pulling the trigger, Bill hit the brakes while Seamus went barreling off the right-hand side of the road without hitting them. His car rolled down a steep embankment, landing in the center of the jersey barrier.

Continuing to drive, Bill saw Seamus was slumped over the steering wheel as Bill continued down the highway, leaving Seamus on the side of the road. Bill was convinced Seamus was dead—no way he survived that crash.

At this point, Tommy was still yelling, "Skipper, what the hell's going on?"

Bill chuckled. "Tommy, you're still there? Threat neutralized. We'll be home in two hours. Saddle up the horses; I don't think it's over."

Tommy replied, "You got it, skipper."

Then Tommy hung up.

Bill said, "Michelle, it's okay, sunshine. Everything's going to be fine. You can put your seat up."

Michelle had tears running down her face. "Dad, what's going on?"

Bill replied, "I've got some things to tell you about my past. That cop who let you go is coming after us. He was using you to get to me."

Michelle asked, "Why?"

Bill replied, "Long story—one I hoped I'd never have to tell you."

Michelle looked puzzled and said, "Did you like kill someone?"

Bill looked over at Michelle, taking his eyes off the road slightly, intermittently checking the rearview mirror to see if a new tail had been acquired, contemplating an explanation.

Finally, Bill said, "This has to do with Jenn and her friend, Owen. Owen's the older brother of Seamus. Owen disappeared the day after BJ's funeral. I didn't kill him, but if I'm honest, nothing would've given me more pleasure. Owen was involved in gun running, drugs, heroin with the Mexican Cartel, as well as kidnapping and murdering BJ. He worked with Colonel Hernandez, as well as Angel Martinez, back when we all served in Iraq. He was my first wife's ex-lover."

Michelle did her vintage Eva reaction, mouth wide open with both hands over her mouth, sitting still for what seemed like five minutes.

Finally, Michelle said, "So this Owen guy—you had something to do with his disappearance, but you didn't kill him?"

Bill replied, "I didn't say anything about having to do with his disappearance. Look, I was happy when he disappeared. Won't deny that."

Michelle looked at Bill ominously. "Well, you inferred it. Disappearing the day after BJ's funeral? Seems like too much of a coincidence. You know, I remember once when I was 12, Angel and the Colonel were talking one afternoon on the deck. They didn't know I was listening. The Colonel talked about a man who delivered that rat-fuck, Owen, and kept referring to this guy as 'Skipper.' Always reliable under pressure."

Bill responded, "Okay."

Michelle replied, "Dad, you're not protecting me by hiding the truth. The call with Tommy—he kept calling you 'Skipper,' which triggered that memory."

Bill thought, should he reply, "Well, that's a coincidence"? Michelle wasn't stupid.

Finally, Bill said, "I'll tell you the whole story under the following conditions."

Michelle replied, "Okay, go on."

Bill said, "1. I'll lay out the story someday soon. It's too complicated to talk about in the car, and I also don't want to be distracted now. 2. When we talk about it, it goes no further than us. There are many things I've never shared. Only Uncle Jack knew the whole story and took it to his grave. 3. For your protection, you'll follow my instructions without discussion until this is over, and I'll tell you when it's over. Remember, when your enemies come, they always come at what you love. 4. Once the story's told, we'll never speak of it again."

Michelle said, "Okay. How much does Mom know?"

Bill replied, "Honestly, I don't know. She rarely spoke about Angel or the Colonel other than to say she thought the Colonel walked on water."

Michelle cut in, "Bullshit, that guy never walked on water. He liked them young."

Bill was a little shocked, asking, "Honey, what'd you mean?"

Michelle had a hardened look on her face, one of resiliency.

Michelle said, "Suffice it to say, if that guy walked on water, it was sewer water on a good day. He liked his companionship young. Turns out, so did Angel."

Bill shook his head, continuing to focus on the road. Before long, they pulled into the driveway in Galveston. Tommy sat on the front porch, reconning the road. Michelle hadn't noticed, but Bill did—Tommy had his AR-15 next to him. As they made it upstairs, Michelle was startled by the guns.

Tommy looked at her. "We got your six, sweetheart. It's going to be okay. Uncle Tommy's here to help."

Bill looked over at Tommy. "All set?"

Tommy replied, "Yep."

Tommy handed Bill his AR-15, saying, "Need to get her secured. An orange car passed by the house twice. Each time, it slowed down as they passed. Reconning."

Bill looked at Michelle. "Michelle, come with me. Upstairs. Let's go!"

When they got upstairs, Bill opened his bedside drawer, pulling out his XDA 45 ACP along with five magazines.

Bill inquired, "Have you ever fired, loaded, or unloaded a weapon before?"

Michelle looked at her dad in shock, shaking her head no.

Bill gave Michelle a crash course, repeating the steps three times.

Bill said, "Show me how to do it. Repeat each step."

Michelle went through the steps, successfully loading and unloading the weapon on the first try.

As Bill headed toward the door, he said, "Don't open this door for anyone unless you hear the safe word, *OMAHA*. That's how you'll know it's safe to open it. Got it? *OMAHA* don't forget. If you don't hear it, and someone tries to open the door, you get down by the end of the bed. Use it as a cover. When the door opens, give him hell—aim three-quarters of the way up the door, then unload on the door. Look, I know you're scared, but you need to overcome that fear. Get comfortable being uncomfortable. My training taught me that, and it's gotten me through a lot of scrapes. Lastly, don't forget to breath."

Michelle was numb at this point. "Be comfortable with being uncomfortable."

She pulled down on the slide, putting one in the chamber, as Bill headed toward the door.

Bill said, "After I leave, lock the door. Whatever you hear downstairs, don't come out until you hear the safe word. Got it? Say it."

Michelle said, "Dad, I heard you."

Bill repeated, "Say it!"

Michelle said, "*OMAHA*!"

Bill left the room; hearing Michelle lock the door behind him. Then, he headed downstairs, where Tommy peered over the railing. When Bill got outside, Tommy motioned his head toward the street. The orange car was back, slowing down again before it passed. Bill had a scope on his AR-15, which revealed four men in the vehicle.

Bill looked at Tommy. "I'm heading downstairs to get a closer look."

Tommy replied, "Got your six from here. I'm a hard target with plenty of firing lanes."

Bill smiled and headed downstairs, taking position near the garage, which provided an obstructed view from the stairs. The orange car crawled down the road, and Bill noticed the windows were now open. He saw three of the men had assault weapons as they drew closer.

As they approached, Bill heard Tommy say from the balcony, "Come on, you bastards!"

Bill remained quiet, but as the car moved past the driveway, he went left around the stairs, outflanking them from behind, having a clear line of sight into the car, while Tommy had them in the kill zone from the front porch. The car stopped at the base of the driveway. The two men from the backseat opened their doors to exit the vehicle, and Bill saw them loading their weapons. However, neither saw Bill.

BANG! Bill took out the first assailant, the one closest to him, with a clean headshot, dropping him to the ground instantly. The second shooter came from the opposite side of the car, heading toward Bill. However, Bill had him in his sights before he could draw down. BANG! One shot, center mass, going down.

For some strange reason, the car didn't take off. It sat there.

Bill moved toward the car. "Hands, put them where I can see them."

They didn't oblige. Tommy heard what Bill said, noticing the same.

Bill yelled, "Last chance!"

The driver panicked, attempting to put the car in drive. However, he only put it in neutral, which only revved the engine. When he revved the engine, Bill unleashed an ungodly hail of bullets, crippling the car and eliminating any further threat. As Bill got closer to the car, he recognized one of the passengers. His face looked familiar, but Bill couldn't place it.

Bill made his way back upstairs, where Tommy came into the house behind him. Bill headed upstairs to get Michelle, but not before Tommy took their weapons and put them back in the safe in Bill's hidden closet downstairs.

Bill reached the bedroom door. "Michelle. *OMAHA*!"

Michelle emerged from the bedroom, coming downstairs visibly rattled.

Tommy looked over at Bill. "What's our story?"

Bill looked at Michelle. "Just got home from Austin. We heard gunfire from down the street as we pulled up to the house; however, it was over when we pulled into the driveway. The car was shot up, so we called 911. Tommy, you took the ride with me to Austin. Michelle, you were asleep in the back seat and didn't see anything. Michelle got the story?"

Tommy said, "I'll call 911 now."

Michelle said, "I got it. I can't wait to hear this story!"

Chapter 1
October 2024

After Michelle's first trip down from Austin, they made plans for a visit to Galveston the following weekend. Bill went up to Austin on Thursday evening to pick her up, as Michelle was off on Friday and needed to be back midday on Sunday. The drive up to Austin was uneventful. As Bill made his way onto the campus, he called Michelle's cell phone to let her know he'd arrived.

Michelle answered, "Hey, Dad. Assuming you're here?"

Michelle calling Bill's Dad choked him up. "Yes, honey. Ready?"

Michelle responded, "I'll be down in two minutes. Just finished packing."

A few minutes later, Michelle emerged from her dormitory, walking across the common area over to Bill's truck.

Bill got out of the truck. "Need a hand?"

Michelle replied, "It's only one bag. I got it, Dad."

Bill took her bag, placing it in the backseat. Before getting in the truck, Michelle gave Bill a great big hug.

Michelle said, "Dad, great to see you. I've got a story to tell you. Can we stop at *Il Tempo* on the ride down?"

Bill replied, "Sure, we can stop there. What's the story?"

Michelle replied, "I'll tell you on the way."

Bill shrugged his shoulders, getting into the driver's side of the truck. As they made their way to the highway, Michelle stared out the window, taking in the sights.

Bill finally asked, "Well, what's the story?"

She began by saying, "You know my friend Amy, Natalie's daughter?"

Bill replied, "Yes."

She replied, "Well, Amy and I've been becoming friends over this semester."

Bill said, "Okay, good, no?"

She replied, "Yes. We've been having a lot of fun."

Bill inquired, "What kind of fun? Good fun, I hope?"

Michelle rolled her eyes like only her mother could. "Yes, Dad. Anyway. Three nights ago, Amy hooked up with a junior named Steve. I met him once but didn't really like him. He seemed stuck-up, only interested in getting into a woman's pants. Amy thinks he's heaven. Are you following me so far?"

Bill replied, "So far."

Michelle continued, "Amy and Steve went to a movie the other night. I don't remember the movie—wait, that's not important. After the movie, they came to a party I was at with some girlfriends. It was kind of a big party; we were blowing off steam from mid-terms."

Bill chimed in, "So what's the significance of them showing up at this party?"

Michelle replied, "Well, when they got there, I saw Amy head to the bar for a drink. Steve followed her. Once she got the drink, I saw Steve put something in her drink when she turned her back to him. There's been a lot of Ecstasy flying around campus."

Bill curiously replied, "What happened next?"

Michelle replied, "I walked over to Amy, ushering her to the ladies' room. She said, 'Let me take my drink,' but I made sure she didn't take a sip. When we got to the ladies' room, I told her what Steve did."

Bill responded, "What happened next?"

Michelle responded, "Well, Amy got very angry, saying she'd fix his wagon. She took the drink, walked over to Steve, turned him around, pretending like she was going to kiss him, and then dumped the drink down the front of his pants. It was funny, it looked like he pissed himself."

Bill replied, "Why do I need to know this? What did Steve do?"

She replied, "Well, Steve made a fist, looking to hit Amy. I saw it coming, so I pushed Amy aside while I drop-kicked him in the ding-ding. I kicked him so hard he threw up as he dropped to his knees. In the end, I got arrested."

Bill thought for a moment, not wanting to overreact. "Couldn't have been too bad, as I'm not picking you up at the police station. Were there charges filed or dropped?"

She replied, "Dropped. Once they knew you were my father."

Bill looked surprised. "How'd I enter into this?"

Michelle responded, "When the policeman detained me, he looked at my student ID and noticed my last name, Quinn. He asked me if I knew Bill Quinn, a former Marine. I told him you're my father. This was after telling him the story about Steve slipping Amy the mickey."

Bill replied, "I'm not getting the connection?"

Michelle replied, "I asked him how he knew you. He said he didn't know you specifically but knew of you. Something to do with Boston, his brother Owen, as well as a woman named Maura. It was almost as if he thought you had street cred. It was kind of cool, to be honest."

Bill sat quietly, continuing to drive, starting to think about Boston.

Bill asked, "What was the policeman's name?"

Michelle replied, "Seamus DeValera. Like the first Irish president, but no relation."

Bill replied, "Honey, I don't know him."

Michelle said, "Dad, he knew you. Any daughter of yours was a friend of his he told me. When Steve got back to the dorm, he came up to our room to apologize to Amy. Clearly, he was beaten again. He had a bruise on his jaw, a welt over his left eye, and was still walking very funny. Almost like he'd been kicked in the ding-ding again."

Bill said, "What's going to happen to you? Honestly, that's what matters to me. Does your mother know about this?"

Michelle laughed. "Are you kidding me? She'd freak out and use it as an excuse to visit. That doesn't end well. Besides, she's got her hands full with Espy. As far as the arrest, Seamus tore up the report in front of me, then let me go."

At this point, Bill shook his head, asking, "Is that it?"

Without saying a word, she smiled, going back to taking in the sights of Galveston. He left the "hands full with Espy" comment alone, not wanting to get involved in Eva's problems. Then, Bill racked his brain about Seamus DeValera, wondering how this connected. Bill thought that when he got home, he'd call Joseph. Perhaps he had a clue about this connection.

Chapter 2
October 2024

Bill and Michelle made their way to the house after stopping at *Il Tiempo* to eat. When they got home, Michelle went into her bedroom, placed her bag on the bed, unpacked, and then laid down on the bed, putting on headphones to listen to music.

Bill said, "I'm going outside to start a fire; join me if you want."

Michelle replied, "I'll be out in a few minutes."

Bill headed outside, poured himself a drink, then started the fire. A few minutes turned into thirty minutes before Michelle finally arrived, having changed into warm pajamas and looking for a blanket. All the while, Bill was thinking about the story Michelle dropped on him on the ride home.

As she settled in on the couch, she asked, "Dad, what do you want to talk about this weekend?"

Bill replied, "A couple of things, but it'll wait until tomorrow. I'm a little tired from all the driving. Let's chill out this evening. Okay?"

Michelle yawned slightly. "That's fine."

Within a few minutes, she was asleep on the couch while Bill enjoyed his drink, staring into the fire. It was getting late in the evening, but Michelle's story was picking at him. Bill thought, should he call Joseph? It was 23:30 in NYC. Michelle was asleep, so Bill figured, why not call Joseph?

Joseph answered, "Hey, Billy Boy! How's things?"

Bill replied, "Fine, hope all's well."

Joseph responded, "Things are good, but we miss you."

Bill said, "Great. Look, I've got a favor to ask. My daughter's involved in a scrape, arrested for standing up for a friend in a bar. The interesting thing is the cop let her go, saying he knew me."

"His name was Seamus DeValera. I don't know who he is. I knew Owen was a DeValera."

Joseph sat silent for a moment, taking in what was shared.

After a long pause, Joseph said, "I'm going to my office, hang on."

Bill replied, "Okay."

Bill heard Joseph making his way through the bar to the office, once Uncle Jack's office.

Finally, Joseph said, "Okay, I'm alone. Billy boy, run me through this again."

Bill repeated the story, or at least what Michelle told him. Bill said "This cop seemed to be doing her a solid."

When Bill finished, Joseph said, "Billy boy, only you can find this kind of trouble."

Bill, a little surprised, asked, "What's that mean?"

Joseph replied, "Wish we could talk face to face. The cop is Owen's youngest brother. Also, he's no cop—he's a rent-a-cop, a dirtbag too."

Bill was stunned, thinking he couldn't get away from this family.

Bill said, "What now? He knows my daughter; mentioned Boston and Maura to her. If he touches my daughter, you won't be able to identify him with dental records."

Joseph calmly stated, "Calm down, we'll work this out. I'll send someone to Austin to review the situation. Stand down, I'll get the word out: she's my niece. It will be taken care of."

Bill replied, "Is this guy looking for retribution?"

Joseph replied, "Let's not go into that until we're face to face. Can you come tomorrow?"

Bill responded, "No. I've got Michelle for the weekend. I don't want her involved in this any more than she already might be. I'm taking her back on Sunday, so I'll set up a flight for Sunday afternoon."

Joseph responded, "That works. I'll send someone down to assess the situation before we get together. You said this cop's name was Seamus DeValera?"

Bill responded, "Affirmative. I'll make my arrangements tomorrow morning."

Joseph responded, "Sounds like a plan. See you soon."

Then Joseph hung up. Bill went back to the side of the deck where the fire was. Michelle was fast asleep while the fire was dwindling. Bill put another log on the fire, poured four fingers of his new favorite bourbon, Horse Soldier Bourbon, then lit a Nat Sherman cigar. His mind was racing. He thought he trusted Joseph, but he was no Uncle Jack. As Bill puffed on his cigar, Michelle woke up.

Michelle said, "Dad, I'm heading into bed. Is everything okay? I thought I heard you mumbling. Were you on the phone?"

Bill responded, "Honey, you were fast asleep. Go to bed. We'll talk more in the morning. I'm so happy you came down."

Michelle smiled, heading inside toward her bedroom. Bill stayed on the deck, enjoying his refreshments as well as the fire. The wind made it cool. He began to think back to Boston, which was 30+ years ago. Bill was getting concerned about how this might impact Michelle, beginning to feel angry.

About halfway through the cigar, Bill recalled what Joseph said. *Calm down, we'll get this sorted.* Also, Bill thought about how Uncle Jack may have handled this call, coming quickly to the realization—that Joseph was no Uncle Jack.

Chapter 3
October 2024

The next morning, Bill awoke early, deciding to take a walk on the beach. When he got downstairs, Michelle was still asleep, so he went down to the beach, walked east for 30 minutes, then turned back toward home. Upon returning, Michelle was up, having made a pot of coffee.

Michelle said, "Dad, I made coffee. Want some?"

Bill replied, "Sure. When did you want to have our chat?"

Michelle said, "What chat?"

Bill responded, "The chat! You know, the whole reason you came for the weekend."

Michelle replied, "Oh, sorry, still waking up."

Bill quipped, "Just like your mother. Anyway, we need to talk about finances. You need to understand this: God forbid anything happens to me. You'll need to be versed in this, as I don't want any disruption to your schooling or your future. Lastly, I want this to stay between us. Perhaps in the future, you could share it with your spouse, assuming you trust them. There's a lot of money at stake."

Michelle was a little surprised by Bill's approach. This was the first time they really talked about this, with an assertive side of Bill

Michelle had never seen before. Bill understood this was new to her, but this was about her future, so he was going to make it as simple as possible but clear on how important this was.

Michelle asked, "Can I share this with Mom?"

Bill replied, "I'd rather not, after what's happened. If you want, you can talk about it in general. I never got the impression that she managed investments. Her knowing is fine, but if I'm alive, I'd rather this stays between us. You're now the sole beneficiary. There's nobody else."

Michelle responded, "Okay, I understand."

Bill took her through the investments, locations, and amounts in each account, explaining why he'd invested the accounts the way he did and, most importantly, how to access the accounts if he was dead. The last statement was hard for her, as he could tell by the look on her face—*he just came into my life, and now they're talking about his death*. Bill recognized it was a morbid topic, but she needed to be prepared. That was more important.

Bill told her, "This isn't the only time we'll cover this. It's a lot to take in."

Michelle said, "Thanks. It is a lot to take in, but I see how important it is. Why do you have so many accounts in the US and Switzerland?"

Bill replied, "Various reasons. Some were beneficial tax-wise, while some were well established overseas funds. Remember, this is an investment in your future, not play money. College, buying a house, dividends to live on, emergency funds."

Bill didn't get into the specifics regarding the funding of each account, as he didn't see the point. Also, Bill didn't want to get into his sordid history, not wanting to burden her with more. His focus was on what was relevant for her future. With all this hanging in the air, Michelle looked at the details of the accounts, evaluating the investments and amounts.

Michelle said, "Impressive portfolio. How'd you amass this fortune?"

Bill smiled. "A lot of hard work. I was a saver. Sometimes, too frugal, but that's the way I was raised. If you've got money, at the very least, you can choose your own misery. Without it, your choices are limited."

Michelle chimed in, "What about happiness?"

Bill replied, "Happiness is a state of mind, in my opinion. Money's not the only thing; however, it can really help when you need it. One last thing—perhaps somewhere in your future, you'll want to get married. To protect yourself, especially with the size of this portfolio, consider a prenuptial agreement. I know it sounds strange when you love someone, but it prevents a lot of heartache later if it doesn't work out. The advisor is aware of this. In the event I pass, use him as a sounding board for whatever you do. That's why he gets paid."

Bill saw Michelle getting depressed from the conversation. It's always hard to talk about death, especially when Michelle had her whole life ahead of her. Also, given their situation—the fact they'd only known for a month that she was his daughter—it made it hard to hear all this.

Bill ended the conversation. "Let's take a break; let it sink in. We've got time to work our way through it."

Michelle looked relieved. "Walk on the beach? I'll get changed. I know you walked earlier, but we could head down and enjoy the sun."

Bill replied, "Sure, let's go."

The wind was strong, coming in from the southeast. As they walked into the wind, it made it hard to carry a conversation, but Bill recognized Michelle was processing the information he shared, hoping it wasn't overwhelming her. Despite its importance, he noticed a pensive side of her he hadn't seen before.

They walked on the beach for 45 minutes, soaking in the sun, working up a little sweat, and enjoying the leisurely sounds of the

Gulf. Bill surmised the walk was helping Michelle's mood as she enjoyed the sun on her face, as well as the roaring sound of the ocean.

Chapter 4
October 2024

Bill hadn't heard from Joseph by Sunday morning. He needed to get Michelle back to Austin, so they headed out around 08:00, hoping to beat the traffic. He also planned to take Michelle out for a nice lunch before heading back for his flight to New York.

When they got in the car, Michelle settled into the passenger seat, going back to sleep. It always amazed him—this generation seems to sleep a lot. When Bill was that age, he was always on the move. Instead of fighting it, he put on some *King George* and cruised up I-45.

About an hour into the car ride, Michelle woke up. "Dad, how much longer?"

Bill replied, "Probably 90 minutes, maybe a little more if we hit traffic. Why?"

Michelle replied, "I wanted to let Amy know what time I'll be back. I've got a sneaking suspicion she had a guy over last night. She posted about her new boyfriend on X."

Bill asked, "Is that a problem?"

Michelle responded, "I like her, but she's way too forward with men, falling in love at the drop of a hat. Personally, she's got Daddy issues."

Bill responded, "Well, that's her issue. You don't need to get caught up in her problems. It's not affecting your schoolwork, is it?"

Michelle replied, "Dad, I know you're right, but it's hard when you must have an alternative place to go at night because she's hooked up. One time, a man was leaving our room—*not a college student.* When I went into the room, I saw a stack of $100 bills on her dresser. When I asked later, she said the guy owed her money, came by to drop it off, and then they hooked up."

Bill came back with, "That's a lot to handle. Tried to talk to her or your RA?"

Michelle responded, "I did talk about it with her once, but she played it off as nothing. Since then, she's been out every evening instead of sleeping in our room. Also, she's been acting strange. When she comes home, she reeks of weed. She's a friend, so it's got me worried for her."

Bill responded, "Like I said. Those are her demons, not yours. Stay focused on you. Have you said anything to your mom about this?"

Michelle replied, "Yes. But even Mom gave me a similar response. 'Talk to the RA.'"

At this point, Bill didn't know what to say. Also, he wondered if he should say anything to Natalie about this. Amy was Natalie's stepdaughter, and he knew their relationship had been strained even before her husband died, getting worse after his death.

Amy's father was out of the picture, leaving Natalie in charge of his estate and providing funds for Amy's schooling. Amy had an inheritance allotted to her, but she couldn't touch any of it until her 30th birthday. Natalie had asked Bill to look over the estate paperwork and even attend a meeting with her advisor, giving Bill this additional insight. With that said, Michelle didn't need to know about that. She'd have her own inheritance to deal with once Bill was gone.

As Bill continued to drive, he thought about Fatima and Eva, as his mind drifted. When they went to Tommy's house the day Bill found out about Michelle, he told Tommy that he had heard from Fatima many years ago, apologizing for not saying sooner. He also told Tommy that his special friend from the UK was involved in finding her. Eventually, Bill told the story of Fatima—effectively a homage to Fatima—putting Eva into a jealous fit when they are alone later.

Eva continued her jealous fit into the next day, bitter that she wasn't the center of attention for some strange reason. Bill got angry about Eva's reaction, not understanding the jealousy over a woman he hadn't seen in 30+ years, who was married and a grandmother. Bill and Eva had a massive blowout, both vowing they were finished.

Two weeks was all it took for things to fall apart again. He guessed she didn't envision much after all. Michelle was disappointed but also understood the crazy shit her mother was doling out, or so she said. Bill started across the 6th Street bridge, heading up toward UT.

As they got to Michelle's dormitory, Bill asked, "Want to get something to eat?"

Michelle said, "Dad, I'd love to, but I've got studying to do. I took the weekend off, so I need to put some time in this afternoon."

He felt proud, schoolwork came before lunch with Dad.

Bill said, "Okay. I'll help you inside, then head out."

Michelle smiled. "Dad, I've only got one bag. You can drop me off. This way, you can beat the traffic. I know how you hate traffic. Besides, if Amy's got a visitor, I'm sure that'll be awkward. I would hate to see you in that position with her or Natalie."

It was hard to argue with her logic, so Bill said, "Makes sense. Love you."

Michelle replied, "Love you too!"

Bill dropped her off, waving goodbye as she walked into the dormitory. As he saw the door close behind her, Bill started to think about the path home, as well as a stop for something to eat. There was a great roadside place on Highway 71, *Hruska's*, with awesome sandwiches and homemade cookies. The sausage sandwich with mustard was a favorite. As he headed back over the 6th Street bridge, his phone rang. It was Eva.

Bill picked up. "Hey, just dropped Michelle off. Everything okay?"

Eva replied, "Why do you ask me that every time I call?"

Bill coldly replied, "It's just a question. What can I do for you?"

Eva said, "Everything's fine. I just got off with Michelle. She told me what a wonderful weekend you had. Told me about her college fund. I wanted to say thank you for being there."

Bill replied, "That's my job. It's great she appreciates it. A testament to how her mother raised her up."

Eva responded, "Nice of you to say. How are you? Are things going well for you?"

Bill hesitated, then Eva asked, "Too uncomfortable?"

Bill replied, "Look, I don't want to fight. I want us to be friends so we can be there for Michelle's sake. I'm sorry things went south, for what that's worth."

Eva replied, "Makes sense. At a minimum, I want us to have that for Michelle's sake. Michelle mentioned you're dating someone. How's that going?"

Bill was a little surprised at all this interest in his life.

Bill asked, "Are you sure you want to hear about this? I'm tap dancing a little, as I appreciate why you might be asking, but I don't want to cause you any pain. I hope you know what I mean."

Eva took a moment. "I understand you're not looking to hurt me. I know you've had so much pain in your life. I thought talking to an outsider might help. Does that make sense?"

Bill chuckled. "I'm going to be a little snarky for a second. So, my ex-girlfriend wants to help me with my new girlfriend? Is that my takeaway?"

Eva laughed before replying, "Despite you prefacing it, you're an ass. Thought we could be friends and help each other out when needed. I'm not trying to pry myself back into your life."

Bill responded, "Really?"

Eva sat quietly for almost a minute.

Bill said, "Sorry, I was trying to be funny—her name's Natalie. As a matter of fact, Michelle's roommate, Amy, is her stepdaughter. We started dating two weeks after our blowout. So far, it's been fine. She is interesting and pretty. We have a lot of fun when we're together."

Eva said, "That's nice. Is it serious? Have you told your daughter all about it?"

Bill replied, "I've told Michelle a little, but I think she's fantasizing we'll get back together if I'm honest. I haven't shared all the details with her yet, but if this moves toward a deeper relationship, I'll tell her more. Don't worry, I won't provide all the details. Some details don't need to be shared. Besides, Natalie has her hands full with Amy. I'll just leave it at that."

Eva replied, "That's nice it's going well. I think you should tell her more. Listening to you talk about her, I can tell in your voice she means something to you. Don't be afraid to take a chance."

Bill asked, "What about your love life? Anyone of interest in your life?"

Eva became evasive, hedging her response. "Well, I've dated some frogs but haven't found a prince yet. Had one a long time ago but let him slip through my fingers. I'm good being alone right now."

Bill replied, "Well, don't be afraid of it. Take your time, do your homework."

Eva said, "Thanks. Hey, I've got to run. It's nice catching up. Let's speak soon."

Bill replied, "Okay."

Then Bill hung up the phone.

Before he realized it, Bill was coming up on Hruska's. The place was empty for a Sunday afternoon as he made his way to the counter to order a sausage sandwich with mustard. It's a slightly smoked sausage with pecan wood, served on homemade rye bread, with mustard optional, but very tasty with it. Bill grabbed an iced tea as well as a package of oatmeal raisin cookies.

As Bill sat down with his sandwich, he thought about the weekend with Michelle, all the stories she told, and the phone call from Eva. Bill was suspicious of Eva's angle. He never thought they'd be friends after everything that's happened. Bill questioned if she was being genuine.

Before long, Bill decided to be cautious about talking to her about things not related to Michelle.

Chapter 5
Early November 2024

After Tommy called 911, the police arrived quickly. It appeared none of the neighbors had called, as no one was outside waiting when the police showed up. When the officers arrived, they stuck to their story, being questioned separately and then brought together when their accounts lined up.

The policeman said, "We've gotten complaints about an orange car in the area over the past few days. Have you seen the car before today?"

Bill replied, "No, can't say I have. I've been up in Austin over the past few days, so I've not been here much. What's the significance of the orange car?"

The policeman looked annoyed by the question. "Thanks, that's all I need."

Bill responded, "Sure. Happy to help."

The policeman glared at Bill, walking off to his patrol car while a wrecker arrived to remove the car from the street. The wrecker driver waited for over an hour before the coroner agreed to move the bodies, not before the police detectives finished taking scene photos. Tommy, Michelle, and Bill were huddled in the driveway, watching as things unfolded.

Bill asked Michelle, "Are you okay?"

Michelle didn't say a word but nodded no.

Bill walked over to the policeman. "Is it okay if we head upstairs?"

The detective in charge walked over. "What's your hurry?"

Bill responded, "Not in a hurry, it's warm standing in the sun. We live right here, so pop upstairs if you need anything."

The detective looked at Bill. "You live right here, you say?"

Bill replied, "Yes."

The detective said, "Go ahead. You didn't see anything?"

Bill responded, "Nothing more than what we told the patrolman."

The detective didn't like Bill's attitude, but he seemed to accept his response before they headed upstairs. As they got upstairs and inside, Michelle lost her footing, almost fainting.

Bill grabbed her before she hit the floor. "Honey, you okay?"

Michelle replied, "Dad. I know one of the guys in the car."

Bill responded, "What? How do you know them?"

Michelle started to cry. "Marco. Mom's godson."

Bill was shocked. Tommy sat down, putting his hands over the back of his head. Bill recalled his face—the young man on his NYC porch the last time Bill saw the Colonel. That was the same kid with Hernandez.

Michelle leaned into Bill, sobbing. "We killed him."

Bill responded, "Marco chose to be in the car. They were here to kill us. Don't ever lose sight of that. Cousin or no cousin, it was them or us."

Michelle sat quietly as the effects of the moment hit her like a ton of bricks. She'd start to cry, then compose herself. After another 30 minutes, the police and the coroner were gone.

Michelle looked out the window, asking Bill, "Dad, how do we tell Mom?"

Bill softly replied, "I'll tell her delicately. Why would he be involved with this?"

Michelle replied, "I don't know."

Tommy said, "Skipper if Seamus wasn't in the car, why hasn't he shown his face?"

Bill replied, "Great question. This isn't over. I can't get away from this fucking family."

Michelle interrupted, "Dad, I'm going in to lie down."

Bill nodded as Michelle went to her room. Tommy and Bill sat on the couch, staring at the carpet for a while. Bill thought of Michelle's safety, as well as why the hell Joseph hadn't called.

Bill looked over at Tommy. "I'm going outside to make a call."

Tommy replied, "Joseph?"

Bill nodded, grabbing his phone and heading out to the deck. Bill rang him. Joseph picked up on the first ring.

Joseph said, "Billy Boy. How's tricks?"

Bill replied, "Not good. Let me tell you about it."

Joseph quietly sat as Bill went through the story—doing battle in the street, dealing with the police, and the revelation that one of the men was Eva's godchild.

When Bill wrapped up, Joseph said, "Sounds like you still got it. I don't see what the problem is. You know Marco was the Colonel's godson. Like the Colonel—a real piece of shit. Billy boy, I should hire you to deal with more of my problems."

Bill was stunned by his reaction.

Bill replied, "All I know is Seamus is still out there. You know what I'll do if he gets close to my daughter. He tried running us off the road on a trip back from Austin."

Joseph replied, "Wait. You didn't tell me that!"

Bill responded, "Sorry, I was focusing on the immediate problem. That was next."

Joseph said, "Didn't I call you to tell you he's not a problem? My associate spoke with him, and he assured us this was one big coincidence."

Bill retorted, "Well, that's what he told you, but his actions were different in that car."

Joseph replied, "I'll pay him a visit. Now that I know about this situation, I'll have it dealt with. Unless, of course, he gets to you first. Then feel free to handle it."

Bill said, "I'm glad we spoke. I'll keep Michelle close for now. Also, Michelle was the one who pointed out Marco, so I must tell Eva!"

Joseph said, "Tell her what? Her godson was no better than the Colonel. After the Colonel died, we stopped doing business with all of them. They're cheaters and liars, using too much of their own product. Also, they enjoy being hired guns, real tough guys, and very out in the open, too. In our thing, that's bad for business. Anyway, tell her whatever you want. Why do you care about her?"

Bill replied, "I know the business you're in. When your enemy goes down, it's sometimes a relief. With that said, this is her godson."

Joseph replied callously, "I get it. Handle it however you want."

Bill said, "Okay."

At this point, Joseph hung up while Bill went back inside. Tommy was asleep on the couch while Michelle was sleeping in her bedroom. Bill grabbed a water, sitting down on the couch in silence, contemplating how to tell Eva about Marco.

Chapter 6
Early November 2024

Joseph called the next morning, informing Bill that Seamus had survived the crash. The car had rolled over the jersey barrier, tumbling down a steep embankment and bottoming out in a deep ravine.

At the site, the driver's side of the car faced the sky. When the fire rescue team arrived, the front of the car was engulfed in flames. Firefighters saw Seamus moving inside the vehicle, attempting to punch out the windows. As the firefighters approached, two men were hosing down the front of the vehicle while another firefighter made his way to the top of the car. Seamus was screaming as the temperature inside the car rose to well above 100 degrees.

As Seamus stood on the console, beating on the window, a rain of glass came down upon him as the firefighter smashed the window and then extracted him. As the glass gave way, Seamus pulled himself out with assistance from the firemen, but not before the sudden burst of oxygen drew flames from inside the vehicle, shooting them out the open window.

By the time Seamus made it to the ground, the firemen hosed him down, revealing burns to his legs and arms. Paramedics showed up just as the fireball erupted, racing down the embankment. While the flames were out on Seamus, the burns looked bad, so they sedated him before airlifting him to a local hospital.

While being airlifted, Seamus coded once in route but was revived. Upon arrival, he was rushed directly to the burn unit, where the doctors immediately went to work, removing the burnt clothing he still had on, validating vital signs, and preparing him for treatment. The specialists assessed the severity of the burns, finding that Seamus had second-degree burns on his legs, with serious second-degree burns on his right forearm. By some miracle, his face wasn't affected. While the doctors surmised the burns were severe, they felt he'd make a full recovery, assuming no infection, bandaging the wounds and sedating him to help with the pain.

Joseph and Bill stuck close to each other, monitoring Seamus's progress. Joseph told Bill he had a cop friend who was updating him daily about Seamus. As fate would have it, the cop friend was dating a nurse on the burn unit, easily getting daily updates. As Seamus's prognosis improved, Joseph asked Bill to come to NYC to plot their next move.

After waiting a day and getting unwanted counsel from Joseph, Bill returned Michelle to school. Joseph's associate would keep an eye on her. Bill was apprehensive about Joseph's associate, as well as his attitude. However, Michelle wouldn't be aware she was being watched over.

Joseph called with a daily progress report, while Bill spoke with Michelle daily to keep tabs on her. After arriving in NYC, Bill headed to the Three Aces Pub. It was a good place to go for a beer and a burger—an upscale pub like one you'd see in Ireland. No matter what, the food was fresh.

Bill made his way over from the airport, having the driver drop him off at the bar.

When Bill entered, he said to the bartender, "Excuse me, I'm looking for Joseph."

The bartender replied, "He told us to expect you. He's not here, but he asked me to look after you. What can I get you?"

Bill replied, "A pint of Guinness, a burger medium-rare, and chips."

The bartender responded, "You got it."

The bartender disappeared into the kitchen to place the order, then poured a pint of Guinness and brought it over as Bill sat watching TV. Fifteen minutes later, the bartender showed up with the burger.

The bartender asked, "Need anything else?"

Bill replied, "Another pint, please. Also, ketchup for the burger."

He replied, "Sure thing."

Bill enjoyed his meal, as well as the second pint, waiting for an hour before Joseph came in.

Joseph said, "Billy Boy, let's go in the back. We've got a lot to talk about."

Without allowing Bill to say hello, Joseph escorted him to his office.

When they got into the office, Joseph asked, "Whiskey?"

Bill nodded, replying, "I'll join you."

Joseph poured two glasses, then sat next to Bill in front of Uncle Jack's desk.

Bill asked, "Why are you sitting there?"

Joseph looked at Bill, "You know, Dad's been gone five years. I still have a hard time sitting behind it. You're not the first to comment on that."

Bill replied, "Your dad would've wanted that. You earned it."

Joseph smiled a dry smile. "Thanks. Means a lot coming from you. My dad always had the utmost respect for you: your service, Boston, as well as our other friend."

Bill, surprised, said, "You're buttering me up. What's the punchline? Why am I here?"

Joseph pursed his lips, realizing Bill saw right through his façade. Perhaps some of it was true, but it was too sweet coming from Joseph, knowing full well that Joseph wasn't a kiss-ass. They grew up together, so Bill could always tell when Joseph was blowing smoke.

Finally, Joseph said, "I need your help to take my revenge."

Bill looked ominously at Joseph, having visions of the time he'd heard that from Uncle Jack.

Bill paused for a moment as this rushed through his head. "What revenge? I'm only interested in neutralizing any threat against my daughter."

Joseph looked at Bill. "I got a story to tell you."

Bill thought, *"I've seen this movie before, just a different actor."*

Joseph continued, "Let me finish it before you respond."

Bill replied, "Sure."

Joseph continued, "Do you remember when you came home to sell your place? You had a visitor later that night, the Colonel and his grandson. Remember that?"

Bill broke in, "I do. What's the significance?"

Joseph continued, "I know you knew my dad and Martinez, through the Colonel, had business dealings that went back to Kuwait. When Owen disappeared, the Colonel and Martinez stuck him in a fifty-gallon oil drum, filling it with a mixture of water and acid. Did you know that?"

Bill responded, "All I knew was Owen was dropped off as instructed."

Joseph continued, "Did you know my dad was present at the drop-off?"

Bill looked at him. "I know he was there. Why's that significant?"

Joseph said, "Someone at the drop-off from that day is talking. Juan Tavares sold us out to Seamus. Told him how Owen was delivered and dealt with. Seamus has been in the U.S. for five years, planning a move on all of us."

Bill sat silent for a moment. "Don't know the guy. I'll go through the gates of hell with you, especially if it means protecting my daughter."

Bill pushed back in his mind. Juan Tavares wasn't at his house that day. It was Marco. Marco's dead. Joseph knew that. Something wasn't adding up.

Joseph said, "The reason I was late was we picked up Tavares and handed him over to the Colombians. Now, where you come in—my friends are asking for a favor from you."

Bill glared at him. "Really?"

Joseph coldly looked at Bill. "Take Seamus out. You're right, he used Michelle to get to you. Also, since this prick's still in the hospital, my cop friends have tossed his place and found some interesting things: drugs, a laptop, and pictures of a lot of young girls."

Bill replied, "So, how does that help?"

Joseph replied, "We know where he's been. He's the last of three siblings. The youngest died in a train accident when he was 15. Owen disappeared, of course. Both parents are dead, murdered by the Garda after a robbery that went bad."

Bill responded, "Again, an interesting story. So, if Seamus disappears, all these problems go away?"

Joseph said, "Yes, but there's a twist. Guess who wants him?"

Bill replied, "Let me guess, the Mexicans?"

Joseph responded, "No, the Colombians. Seamus picked up where Owen left off after coming to the States. We boxed out Martinez and the Colonel after Dad died. Seamus was 17 when Owen disappeared. He's bright, ambitious, and very quick with finances, jumping into the family business. However, he thought it'd be better to service his operations with the Colombians rather than the Mexicans. Look. I've got to say, I hate the Colombians—too much violence, total lack of restraint."

Bill responded, "So what's the plan? Not some half-assed drop-off again?"

Joseph said, "I've got a deal set with them. The proposition's sweet—$250 million for this guy. All they want is proof when it's over."

Bill shot back, "Interesting. Don't get me wrong, if it's a choice between protecting my daughter or doing this, it's an easy call. What did he do to deserve this?"

Joseph replied, "They wouldn't tell me. When I asked, the man I spoke with went ballistic—literally incoherent, screaming in Spanish."

Bill replied, "$250 million. How are they getting you that? Be smart; it needs to be placed."

Joseph said, "Swiss bank accounts. You can do whatever you want after that with it."

Bill said, "Didn't know you had that kind of operation. I'm assuming you'll want me to come up with a plan. Also, what's the proposed split?"

Joseph smiled. "My dad took a finder's fee. We've both got a vested interest in seeing this problem eliminated, but since you're doing the heavy lifting, let's say $75 million to me. You'll see $175 million."

Bill replied, "How long do I have to get a plan together?"

Joseph replied, "Do your recon at the hospital. My associates are telling me he's due to be discharged later this week."

Bill responded, "Why the hospital? The whole world knows he's there. Perhaps it's better to handle it in Austin when he returns home?"

Joseph said, "That could work."

Bill replied, "I'll work out the details, then let you know when it's done. What kind of proof? I'm not decapitating this guy's head for their amusement."

Joseph said, "They'll want something but haven't specified. Right now, I need to know if you'll do it."

Bill replied, "Okay. I'll figure it out while I'm constructing a plan."

Joseph asked, "Are you getting Tommy involved?"

Bill paused, thinking, *why would he ask about Tommy?*

Bill downshifted. "No. I need to head to Austin to plan. We'll talk soon."

Bill got up, left the bar, and headed back to the airport for his flight home.

Bill needed to clear his head. Why did Joseph lie about the kid at Bill's NYC home with the Colonel? Why did he seem insistent on having it done at the hospital? Bill thought about whether to get Tommy involved. They'd been through so many scrapes together—was it fair to ask him again? Perhaps Bill would tell him his lone wolf plan, promising to look after Michelle if anything happened.

Bill wrestled with a lot of questions during the flight home.

Chapter 7
Early November 2024

As Bill made his way to the NYC airport, he called Michelle, hoping her sweet voice would calm his nerves.

Michelle picked up on the first ring. "Dad. I'm glad you called."

Bill replied, "Is everything okay?"

Michelle said, "I swear someone's following me."

Knowing she was being followed but not wanting to upset her, Bill figured he would calm her down, unsure if she'd shared this concern with Eva.

Bill responded, "Why do you think that? It's not that Seamus guy, is it?"

Michelle replied, "No. I remember what he looked like, especially after my last trip home. This guy looks like a mob movie character straight out of central casting—black sunglasses, a black leather coat, carrying a newspaper, and at least 100 pounds overweight. I go to the coffee shop. He's there. I head to the commissary on campus; he's there. The fat fuck's everywhere." Bill laughed, responding, "Has he said anything to you?"

Michelle responded, "Not directly, but I overheard him on the phone talking to a guy named Joseph, he kept asking how things were in Brooklyn."

Feeling relieved, knowing it was Joseph's associate, Bill said, "Well, maybe you've got an admirer."

Michelle took a deep breath. "Dad, not funny! What should I do?"

Bill needed to tell her the truth.

Bill said, "Honey, I'm sorry I didn't tell you this. I'm having you looked after for your safety after what happened on Highway 71. The guy works for my cousin Joseph."

Michelle sat quietly for what seemed like an eternity. "You paid someone to watch over me?"

Bill replied, "Yes. It was the best way to protect you without it being me. Joseph's family. In these situations, you trust only blood."

Michelle sighed, saying sarcastically, "Well, at least he's friendly. Dad, I love that you're concerned, but I can take care of myself."

Bill responded, "Honey, I'm not trying to scare you, but this is life and death."

Michelle was a little taken aback. "Life and death?"

Bill replied, "After Highway 71, what happened when we got home that day... Yes, that's abundantly clear."

Michelle responded, "Dad, I trust you. What are we going to do now?"

Bill replied, "I want you to focus on living your life. I'll take care of the rest. Do you hear me? This isn't something you need to worry about."

Michelle started crying. "I'm scared."

Bill replied, "There's nothing to fear. Remember what I've told you. Be comfortable being uncomfortable. My training taught me that. It's gotten me through a lot of scrapes before. Overcome your fear and channel it into always moving forward. It doesn't matter what happens when you're knocked down in life; it only matters what you do when you get up off the mat, dust yourself off, and start moving forward. That's real life. Remember always, I love you, and I'll protect you. No matter what."

Michelle clearly moved and sobbed, "Okay, Dad. I've got to run to class. Can I call later?"

Bill responded, "Sure, honey. Get your head on right for your class. Love you."

Michelle replied, "Love you too."

Bill was waiting for his flight home. While talking to Michelle, Bill decided he needed to talk to Tommy, as he was getting an uncomfortable pit in his stomach. Bill called Tommy, but Tommy didn't answer.

Bill left him a message. "We need to chat when I get back. Be back in the morning."

About an hour later, Tommy texted, "Sorry I missed your call. Got your voicemail mail. Let me know when to stop by tomorrow."

Chapter 8
Early November 2024

When Bill was driving from the airport to Galveston, he called Tommy to let him know he'd be arriving at 12:30. Tommy agreed to meet him. When Bill pulled into the driveway, Tommy was already waiting.

When Bill parked, Tommy asked, "Hey, Skipper, what the hell's going on?"

Bill replied, "Let's go upstairs. Want a whiskey?"

Tommy responded, "It's 12:30, it's that bad?"

Bill didn't respond, heading upstairs with Tommy following. As they got to the top of the stairs, Bill opened the front door, placing his bag inside.

Bill asked Tommy, "Want that whiskey?"

Tommy replied, "Sure. Can't wait to hear this."

Bill went to the inside bar, where he kept the good whiskey, the kind of whiskey that's usually reserved for special occasions. Bill pulled out a bottle of Macallan 18-year-old scotch, pouring two drams. After pouring, Bill placed the glass in Tommy's hand and sat down in the chair directly across from him.

Bill said, "Met Joseph. Apparently, someone from our last mission has been talking."

Tommy jumped up. "What!"

Bill replied, "Yep. Joseph said his name was Juan Tavares. Apparently, he told Seamus about what happened to Owen. Also, Joseph said this kid Tavares was the kid with the Colonel that night in NYC, the day of Uncle Jack's funeral, which is a lie. The kid on my porch was Marco, one of the gunmen in the orange car."

Tommy said, "You've got to be fucking kidding me!"

Bill responded, "Nope, can't make this up. Apparently, Tavares has been passing information to Seamus. Clearly, he's looking to avenge his brother."

Tommy replied, "Understandable."

Bill jumped back in, "Joseph confided that his group picked up Tavares and turned him over."

Tommy shrugged his shoulders. "Interesting. But why's that important?"

Bill responded, "Not exactly sure, but Joseph seemed quite intent on sharing details, almost too eager. If I was paranoid, I swear he was recording our conversation. Regardless, we spent time talking about Seamus and what needed to happen next. I've been getting daily updates on Seamus's progress. Appears he'll be out of the hospital by the end of the week."

Tommy replied, "So what's the plan?"

Bill replied, "Sure you want to be involved? I'm telling you this, so if anything happens to me, you'll look after Michelle. Maybe even Eva. You're the executor of all this until Michelle is 30."

Tommy said, "You'll never have to worry about us looking after Michelle, but you're not doing this alone. Nobody threatens my niece. What's the plan?"

Bill responded, "Thanks. I've been thinking. We need to do some recon. Seamus is still in the hospital, but I've got his address in Austin. Joseph was insisting we do it as Seamus was leaving the hospital, which was strange. It's too public a place, and there are far too many cameras. The whole conversation was strange. He buttered me up with some bullshit before just blurting out, 'Eliminate Seamus.' My radar's been up since I left."

Tommy looked at Bill, a little surprised, seeing Bill was questioning Joseph's loyalty.

Tommy sat silent for a minute. "Do you think he's selling you out?"

Bill didn't say anything at first, but Tommy had seen that look before—the Skipper's 100-yard stare—and surmised Bill was contemplating the same question.

After a short pause, Bill said, "Not sure. I don't trust Joseph. When we do this, I'm sharing only the bare necessities. Once it's done, we make one call: protect our six. The other thing that bothers me are his lies about Marco. I told him about Marco before the trip. A second, his insistence on doing it at the hospital. When I brought up Austin, he gave me a strange look before he said, 'That could work.' Uncle Jack never wanted to know these kinds of details."

Tommy replied, "I hate it when your radar's up."

Bill responded, "Do you think we need to let Amanda in on this just in case anything happens?"

Tommy said, "I'll let her know there's a threat on Michelle we're taking care of. Also, she's to look after Michelle if it goes sideways. I know what to say, so she's not an accessory after the fact."

Bill replied, "Okay. I figured we'd take a trip up, head to the hospital, then Austin, and scope out a few options. At a minimum, if asked, I can say we scoped out the hospital, but it wasn't right."

Tommy replied, "Is this similar to the last drop?"

Bill said, "No. Joseph asked me to take care of it and provide him proof when it's done. For our troubles, we'll be getting $175 million, figuring we'd split it 50:50 when it's done."

Tommy looked at Bill with a look of shock at the amount, then said, "When do we leave?"

Bill replied, "Tomorrow AM. We're going to need to play this coyly with Michelle. We're going to surprise her with a visit, generating our alibis."

Tommy looked at Bill, finishing his whiskey. "You'll pick me up in the morning?"

Bill said, "08:00. Saddle up your horses. We're going to need it."

Tommy smiled, got up from the couch, and made his way to the door. Bill locked the door behind him, then went inside to pack. After packing, Bill prepared his arsenal. Tomorrow morning would come fast. Bill rang Michelle, but she didn't answer.

Five minutes later, she texted, "Hey, Dad, at the library. I'll call tomorrow. Love you."

Bill replied, "Love you too."

Chapter 9
Early November 2024

Joseph called early the next morning, exactly at 05:00 CT.

Bill answered, "Hey, what's got you up so early?"

Joseph responded, "Discharge Friday morning. When are you heading up?"

Bill cautiously replied, "Soon. I'll recon, then make up a plan."

Joseph responded, "Thought we agreed on him walking out the door of the hospital?"

Bill responded, "I'll do a proper recon. You said you're leaving this with me, are you?"

Bill sensed Joseph's frustration with his response, but Bill honestly didn't care. If Joseph wanted Bill to handle it, then let him do it. Otherwise, find someone else.

After a short pause, Joseph nervously said, "You need to get this done, Billy Boy."

Bill said, "If he isn't being released until Friday morning, I'll have until then to get the plan in place. Also, why do you want all the details? Your father never did."

Joseph paused, breathing a little heavier.

Bill finally said, "You still there?"

Joseph replied, "This is awkward, but I need to know the details."

Bill replied, "Why? If you didn't trust me to do this, then why ask me to do it? This seems like a set-up."

Bill heard Joseph trying to compose himself. "We're family. Why would you think that?"

Bill replied, "Your dad never wanted details. If you want me to take care of this, then let me do it."

Joseph replied, "Okay. I'm really hurt you'd say such a thing."

Bill responded, "I'm looking after Michelle's safety. My mind's been racing since I left Brooklyn, with lots of strange things floating in and out."

Joseph said, "Fucking forget about it."

Bill said, "Done. I'll call you when I've got a plan."

Click. Joseph hung up, and Bill went for a shower, just wanting to get clean before heading over to pick up Tommy. Within 30 minutes, he was downstairs, packing his gear in the truck. Bill stowed his gear in the back seat, leaving space for Tommy as well. After loading up with dip, Bill headed over to Tommy's.

When Bill pulled into Tommy's driveway, Tommy was waiting at the bottom of the stairs, his gear next to him.

Bill rolled down the window. "Need a hand?"

Tommy laughed. "I'm not that old yet."

Bill laughed as Tommy opened the rear passenger door, placing his weapons under the bench seat where Bill had made room for him.

Tommy saw the Skoal going in Bill's mouth, then asked, "Got some?"

Bill didn't say a word, handing him the tin of spearmint Skoal. Tommy loaded up as they did in Kuwait, and Bill pulled out of his driveway heading for the main coast road.

Bill asked, "How did things go with Amanda?"

Tommy replied, "She knows the score. She'll look after Michelle if anything happens."

Bill nodded, heading toward I-45 to start the trip up to Austin.

Chapter 10
Early November 2024

Before dealing with the Seamus debacle, Natalie and Bill started spending a lot of time together. Things went south with Eva over her jealousy of Fatima, which Bill still didn't understand. It wasn't like she magically appeared for a visit. Bill wanted to rekindle things with Eva, but perhaps it wasn't meant to be. Perhaps Eva was insulating herself, or maybe Bill was doing Angel's time; either way, it made no sense why she was jealous of a woman she'd never met and probably never would.

The morning after being at Tommy's house, talking about Fatima, Eva woke up very upset.

When Bill came into the bedroom, Eva said, "Maybe you're right, too much water under this bridge."

Bill replied, "I don't understand. You come here, begging for us to take another shot, and a day later, you're jealous of someone who hasn't been in my life for 35 years. A woman who's happily married. You make it sound like she visited, trying to infringe on your territory. Do you hear yourself?"

Eva shut down, saying, "I'm done. I'm going home."

Bill didn't stop her. If Eva wanted to go pout, so be it. Eva's a big girl—however, completely irrational, in Bill's opinion.

As fate would have it, the next morning, Natalie reached out to Bill after Bill had a somewhat heated exchange with Amanda over the fact Bill hadn't called Natalie. Suffice it to say, Bill felt the last 48 hours had been a bit much.

Natalie called. "Hey, it's Natalie. Was hoping we'd catch up?"

Bill replied, "Sorry I haven't called, but the last couple of days have been a lot to take in."

Natalie replied, "I know, Amanda told me. Holy shit! Amanda told me Eva looked deflated when you guys were at her house. Also, Amanda showed me pictures of Michelle—she's beautiful."

Bill said, "Thanks. Would you like to go to dinner tonight?"

Natalie said, "Sure, what should I wear?"

Bill replied, "Something nice but casual."

Natalie DiVincenzo was a slender woman, standing 5'6" and weighing 160 pounds, with brown hair mixed with blonde highlights. Of Italian descent, she had olive oil skin, dark brown eyes, and a wonderful smile. In a word, Natalie was beautiful.

Bill's first date with Natalie was at the restaurant by the inlet across the coast road, a terrific seafood place where Bill had eaten hundreds of times. Bill picked up Natalie for the date, heading over to the restaurant for a 19:00 reservation.

During the first dinner, Bill discovered that Natalie was a woman big into Christmas—an obsession, really. She explained the elaborate decorating she did, which she had been planning since September. Natalie told Bill she'd even driven by his place offering her decorating services. When he saw what Natalie did, Bill felt she went overboard, but in the end, it made her happy.

Things progressed quickly, and they were finishing each other's sentences before the end of the first dinner. The date was three weeks before Thanksgiving.

The Friday after Thanksgiving, Natalie hosted a gathering at Bill's house, while Natalie insisted on the feast of the seven fishes, wanting to dry run Christmas Eve with friends for some strange reason. Bill offered to help with a couple of the dishes, starting a fire outside and cooking the scallops, shrimp, and calamari over an open flame. Natalie made baked clams, crab-stuffed cod, and Zuppa di Pesce.

Suffice it to say, the food was amazing. Natalie invited Tommy, Amanda, Fred, and Mike, as well as their wives. The small party grew into a backyard seafood feast.

Natalie's daughter, Amy, was invited but chose to stay home, which upset Natalie. This became a popular topic as the ladies arrived. However, the ladies distracted her with stories about the four old Marine warhorses, with a healthy injection of wine that helped perpetuate the laughter. The ladies were starting to make Natalie part of their clique.

During the dinner, Bill texted Amy, "Sure you haven't changed your mind? I'll come to get you. I think your mom would be happy if you came."

Thirty minutes later, Amy responded, "I'm good. Thanks for asking. I got other plans."

Bill decided to end it there, having tried for Natalie. Unfortunately, Amy didn't cooperate. They gathered around the table and began the feast. After a short while, the table fell almost silent as everyone ate.

Finally, breaking the silence, Natalie asked, "Everyone's gotten too quiet."

Everyone around the table smiled, giving thumbs up as they continued eating.

Amanda said, "The scallops are great. I love the hickory smoked bacon with it."

The other ladies chimed in about what a triumph the meal was. Bill didn't say anything, as it was Natalie's night, and he didn't want to show her up with his contribution. If asked, all he did was put them over the fire. Natalie was pleased with everyone's reaction to the dinner as well.

For dessert, the ladies each made something. Natalie made Bill's favorite Italian rainbow cookies, figuring Amanda told her these were his favorites. Amanda made a cherry pie, Fred's wife made a Tres Leches cake, and Mike's wife made one of Bill's other favorites—carrot cake.

Suffice it to say, Bill had a sweet tooth, and tonight, he would get his sugar rush. Natalie asked Bill to put coffee on while Bill asked if anyone wanted some whiskey. After dessert, they headed out to the deck, re-stoking the fire, along with whiskey and coffee.

As they sat around the fire, the men raised their glasses, toasting their fallen comrades. The ladies laid back as they toasted, listening to the four old Marine warhorses reminisce about old times. Tommy regaled them with memories going all the way back to boot camp. They were all laughing, clinking whiskey glasses at regular intervals. As the fire burned, libations continued to flow, and everyone enjoyed each other's company with the light breeze from the Gulf. It was a perfect night—mid-50s, cool, crisp, with a ton of stars in the sky.

Around 22:00, the party broke up. Bill went inside to help with the clean-up while Natalie bantered about how successful the night was, thanking Bill for helping.

After the clean-up, they went outside to sit by the fire. Bill didn't turn on the TV, as the sound of the fire was delightful, along with the light ocean breeze. They had a great view of the night sky, curling up under a blanket by the fire getting playful with each other.

Before Bill knew it, Natalie was undoing the button on his pants. In short order, Bill took off Natalie's pants, and they made love for the first time by the fire, wrapped in the blanket for almost 45 minutes. They were interrupted briefly when a car drove by the house, but they had a lot of fun under that blanket.

As they were wrapping up, feeling the fire dwindle, a car pulled into the driveway. They heard some yelling, and then Amy got out of the car. As Amy started toward the stairs, the man in the car got out starting to yell at her. At first, with the wind, it was hard to discern what was being said. When Bill peered over the deck, the man saw him and decided to go back to his car. Amy made her way up the stairs, and Natalie was still putting on her clothes.

Amy said, "Yuck! Really, outside on the porch?"

Natalie hurriedly replied, "What was that all about?"

Amy said, "Mick Collins. Met him in Austin two weeks ago. We met up for dinner. He got annoyed with the waitress and acted like a real ass, so I asked him to take me here. At first, he was going to leave me at the restaurant, but when he saw me ordering an Uber, he said, 'Let me take you home.'"

Natalie asked, "How do you know this boy?"

Amy replied, "Well, he's not a boy, he's 28."

Natalie got a little annoyed. "What's a 28-year-old man want with you?"

Amy said, "Met him through a friend, Seamus. He happened to reach out this afternoon about dinner. I thought it'd be nice, as I wasn't interested in being here. No offense."

Natalie got angry. "You'd rather spend time with some guy you hooked up with at school than with people who love you!"

Amy coldly looked at Bill. "Can you drive me home? I only came here because I didn't want to bring him to Mom's house alone."

Bill responded, "Sure, let me get my keys. Natalie, need anything while I'm over there?"

Natalie said, "Yes. Please, grab the bottle of wine in the fridge."

Looking at Natalie, a little puzzled, Bill went inside to get his keys to take Amy home.

When they got in the car, Bill asked Amy, "Look, I know you two don't get along, but you realize she cares about what happens to you. I've heard her talk numerous times about how detrimental your behaviors have been since you left for school."

Amy sat there, saying nothing. Fortunately, Natalie's place was 5 minutes away, while it was clear Amy had shut down. When they reached Natalie's place, Bill went inside to retrieve the wine.

After grabbing the wine, Bill said, "Have a good night. Lock the door behind me."

Amy said, "Goodnight, thanks for the ride."

As Bill walked downstairs, he saw a car parked down the road. As he made his way back toward his place, he passed by the car but saw it was empty. With that, he made his way back home. When Bill returned, Natalie was sitting by the fire, adding two more logs while Bill was gone, and had poured two whiskies.

When Bill noticed the whiskey glasses, he asked, "You okay?"

Natalie smiled slightly. "That girl's going to be the death of me."

As Natalie was talking, Bill sat down next to her, sipping his whiskey and assessing she was unwinding after what had transpired. A few minutes later, Natalie was sound asleep next to Bill on the couch as the last whiskey finished her off. Bill sat on the couch next to Natalie while she slept, watching the fire and thinking about the animosity between Amy and Natalie, reflecting that Amy didn't go back to school for a couple of days.

Chapter 11
November 2024

Bill needed to call Eva about Marco, a conversation he wasn't looking forward to for two reasons. One, he didn't know how Eva would react to the news. Second, he dreaded rehashing what happened in Galveston on her last trip, opening all the old wounds. He wasn't sure he could handle such drama today.

Bill texted Eva: *"Free to chat? There's something we need to talk about."*

Eva called Bill instantly. "What's wrong? I've had a bad feeling all day."

Bill replied, "Did Michelle talk to you about her last visit to Galveston?"

Eva responded nervously, "No. What's going on?"

Bill responded, "It's a little involved, so I need you to let me get through it first."

Eva said, "Okay, but I can't promise you that. You, of all people, know that."

Bill told Eva the story—the trip back from Austin, Seamus' antics, the gunfight at the house in Galveston, where they were questioned by the police, and then Michelle revealed to Bill that she knew one of the gunmen, Marco. Surprisingly, Eva was quiet while telling the story.

When Bill wrapped up, Eva said, "Honestly, not shocked. Marco took a bad turn when the Colonel died. Anyway, what happens now? You're protecting Michelle, right?"

Surprised by her lack of emotion, Bill replied, "I'm always protecting Michelle. I'm going up to Austin for business and planned on surprising her. I'll reach out if I need anything, but I won't go into the reasons why."

Eva responded, "I'm not sure I want to know more than that, do I?"

Bill responded, "No. I've made provisions for Michelle in the event something happens. If it does, you may be hearing from Amanda."

Eva nervously chimed in, "Bill, you're scaring me."

Bill replied, "It's probably nothing. Best you don't know what happens next, but I do want you to know Michelle will always be safe."

Eva came back, "Have you told Michelle any of this?"

Bill said, "Yes and no. She knows about the investments and how to access them. I haven't told her there's a letter for you, her, Tommy, and Amanda if something happens to me. They're suggestions about how to proceed without me, as well as looking after Michelle's future."

Eva replied, "None of us are ready to lose you!"

Bill responded, "I'm not ready for that either, but if it's my life or protecting our daughter, it's a simple choice. In any event, I wanted to outline my wishes clearly."

Eva then asked, "Is there anything else? Anything I need to know?"

Bill replied, "No. I can't think of anything but be prepared for a call or two over the next couple of days. If you don't get one, don't be nervous. You've got to act like nothing's wrong with Michelle."

Eva replied, "OK. I'll do whatever you need me to. Please make sure Michelle's ok. I can't bear to lose her."

Bill said, "That's my number one priority. I'd better go now. Talk soon."

Eva said, "Yes, talk soon. I love you."

Bill was a little taken back by her last statement, not knowing what to say to her. The silence was awkward for a few moments.

Bill said, "I appreciate what you're doing to help. Talk soon."

Then Bill hung up. He couldn't bring himself to say those words to Eva in the moment. Bill hated to admit there was a part of him that still cared, but that was over now. His focus needed to be on Michelle, concentrate on what mattered in the moment.

Also, what Eva didn't know was Natalie had come up the stairs just as they wrapped up the call. Fortunately, the wind was blowing hard, making it impossible to hear any conversation from the staircase. Eva didn't know Tommy would be heading up with Bill, establishing an alibi if necessary. Bill was intent on not providing too many details to avoid anyone becoming an accessory after the fact. This was a need-to-know basis, and Eva didn't need to know.

Bill outlined a plan of attack, knowing full well what Joseph wanted. From Bill's experience, the hospital was too risky and difficult to execute. Even without seeing the layout of the hospital, it was clear that security would be tight, with cameras everywhere. On the surface, outside the hospital wasn't a potential successful target.

As a second option, Bill considered going into the hospital, disguised, and confronting Seamus in his room. Maybe Tommy could provide a diversion, perhaps setting off a fire alarm to occupy hospital security. However, as Bill thought through this, it involved going directly into the hospital, and the security inside would be tight, with cameras recording 24/7. It'd be easier to take Seamus out outside the hospital than inside.

The third option was Austin. Bill thought of the benefits of handling it this way. One, they'd recon Seamus's place, be able to surveil, and find easy access in and out to the building. They'd have easy access to hotels and easy getaway options.

The more Bill thought about it, the more he felt this would be the best option, with the highest chance for success. Bill wanted to lay out the options for Tommy and get the great tactician's thoughts. Given his involvement, it was only fair to get his input.

Bill called Tommy. "When can you stop by?"

Tommy said, "Game planning?"

Bill replied, "Yep. I've got a few ideas but wanted to lay them out with you."

Tommy replied, "I'll be over in 30."

True to his word, Tommy was at Bill's front door in 30 minutes.

Bill opened the door. "Want anything?"

Tommy responded, "No. I'm good. Let's get to work."

They made their way to the kitchen counter, where Tommy saw Bill had done a few scenarios before Tommy showed up. Bill walked him through each of the scenarios. As Bill walked through each of them, it was clear Tommy had similar opinions.

When Bill ended with option 3, he asked, "Is there something else you can think of or something I've missed?"

Tommy replied, "So far, this makes sense. I agree with you. The first two are too difficult to execute and too risky. Option 3 sounds best, it's private, if you know what I mean."

Tommy and Bill headed out for Austin the next morning.

Chapter 12
November 2024

As Tommy and Bill made their way to Austin, both were very quiet, each seemingly getting their battle stares on. This wasn't their first rodeo; however, this had a different intensity to it—Michelle was involved. If they failed, she could be hurt or even killed, a thought that drifted in and out of Bill's head on the trip up.

They stopped at Hruska's for a bite to eat before heading to the hospital. After finishing, they made their way to the hospital.

As they pulled up, Bill parked in a vacant lot across the street. Tommy pointed out that the parking lot didn't have cameras, based on what he observed. They took out binoculars beginning their homework, despite both thinking the hospital wasn't going to work. They looked at the front of the hospital, the side entrances, and the main lobby. Bill pointed out where the cameras were, while Tommy pointed out the security details. After 90 minutes, they noticed a pattern to the security patrols—making it clear, some of the security guards were retired police officers. Many had weapons, and while not uncommon in Texas, it was clear these weren't run-of-the-mill security guards. Tommy and Bill had seen enough after two hours. This wasn't the place. Then, they headed to Austin.

Arriving in Austin, they pulled up to Seamus's apartment, parking across the street to assess if any cameras were surveilling the area. It became clear within minutes that this place didn't have cameras. It was a courtyard-style apartment with several exits. The walkways appeared to have lights, but there were only a few streetlights inside the courtyard.

After 15 minutes, they made their way across the street for a closer look, even moving up to Seamus's apartment. Bill made his way around the backside of the street, positioning himself to get a better vantage point of the target. Additionally, he was able to scope out a more secluded area to park when they executed. When Bill got into position, he motioned to Tommy, who came up the front walkway.

When Tommy got to Seamus' door, he noticed a Ring doorbell, so he backed off, heading back downstairs. Ok, the first impediment to overcome, but nothing serious. While Tommy made his way back to the truck, Bill swung around to the front of the apartment, heading for the truck.

Bill got inside the truck with Tommy. "Other than the Ring doorbell, see anything else?"

Tommy replied, "No, it should be a slam dunk."

Bill was a little surprised at his response. "Nothing's a slam dunk until it is. Here works. What do you think?"

Tommy replied, "Agreed. Once we get him, what are you going to do to him?"

Bill smirked. "We'll think of something. Need Joseph's input on that. Let's call him."

With that, Bill picked up his phone and rang Joseph.

Joseph picked up on the first ring. "Billy Boy. Done?"

Bill replied, "Just finished recon. We've got a plan. Got a question: how do you want this done?"

Joseph replied, "I'm not sure what you mean?"

Bill said, "Do you have a preferred method? Does it need to appear a certain way?"

Joseph said, "No. Just proof. That's our ticket if you know what I mean."

Bill replied, "Got it. Still on track for Friday?"

Bill heard a click on the phone.

Joseph shot back, "Friday, when and where's this happening?"

Bill responded, "I'll call you when it's a rainy night in Dublin."

Joseph laughed. "You and my dad, those fucking code phrases."

Bill shot back, "I'll talk to you."

Then Bill hung up the phone. Tommy heard Bill's side of the conversation, knowing it didn't matter how. All that mattered was that it happened.

Tommy said, "Hey, when's this guy getting released?"

Bill replied, "Still Friday morning."

It was Wednesday afternoon, so they had another day to prepare, along with establishing alibis, if necessary. It was 16:00, so they decided to head over to the hotel, which was not far from UT. Once Bill got settled in the room, he called Michelle to surprise her, letting her know he was in town.

Michelle said, "Nice surprise, Dad. Can't wait to see you."

Bill said, "We'll be over in 30. Dinner out, you choose the place."

Michelle said, "OK."

The boys picked Michelle up, heading to the restaurant she chose. It was a little Italian bistro not far from campus. The conversation was casual, and Bill thought Michelle might be recovering from a hangover. She mentioned she'd been out with friends the night before.

Bill asked Michelle, "You weren't alone with anyone, were you?"

Michelle replied, "No, Dad, with some girlfriends. It started out with, 'Hey, I'm in the mood for a beer,' then it wound up with five of us and a case of beer."

Bill nodded, giving his best fatherly disapproving look. Michelle smiled as if to say, *you remember when you were in school, right?* Tommy sat silent the whole time, laughing, mostly at Bill's reactions, finding it amusing watching his old pal struggle with newfound fatherhood.

As dinner wrapped up, they paid the check and took Michelle back to her dormitory. They watched as she headed in the door. From there, they went back to Seamus's apartment for a nighttime recon.

As they got 500 yards from Seamus's place, they parked the truck and walked down to the apartment complex. Tommy and Bill were walking next to each other with their XDA 45ACP pistols at their sides. Luckily, it was cool that evening, making it easy to conceal the weapons with their jackets.

As they made their way toward the courtyard, the lighting was perfect. Just as they suspected, it was a dark courtyard with dimly lit walkways. They made their way up the staircase to the third-floor balcony. As they got to the top of the stairs, Seamus's apartment was on the corner, giving them easy access. Turning off the Ring doorbell wouldn't be a problem, Bill thought.

Tommy suddenly stopped. "Hear that?"

Bill whispered, "Yep, sounds like someone's watching TV. There's a slight opening in the curtain. I'll look in, cover my six."

Tommy gave Bill a thumbs up while Bill headed toward the window, peering in. There was someone watching TV, a girl, who was talking on the phone. Also, Bill saw on the table what appeared to be bricks wrapped in brown paper, stacks of them, sitting on the table just to the right of the TV.

Suddenly, the woman walked into the living room, having hung up, and all the talking stopped. As she got closer to the window, Bill recognized the girl. It was Amy. *What's she doing here?*

Tommy whispered, "Hey, Skipper, what's going on?"

Bill moved away from the window slowly. "Let's go, we've got another complication."

Tommy and Bill headed back to the truck. After starting the truck, Bill pulled away quickly.

Tommy replied, "What did you see?"

Bill responded, "Drugs stacked on a table next to the TV. The girl we heard was Amy—Natalie's stepdaughter."

Tommy slowly shook his head. "You can't make this shit up. So, what's the plan?"

Bill said, "Let's head back to the hotel. Amy adds a complication we need to think about."

Tommy and Bill headed back to the hotel, needing a stiff drink and a quiet corner to plan. The thing worrying Bill was how to extract Amy from this situation. Tommy and Bill made it to the bar, ordering two stiff bourbons, and found a quiet table away from the rest of the bar to chat.

Tommy asked, "So Skipper, got a plan yet?"

Bill replied, "We need a diversion to get Amy out of there. But what?"

Tommy chimed in, "Could pretend we're the police, a raid. You said you saw drugs."

Bill responded, "That's got promise, but it can't be either of us. Clearly, she knows us."

Tommy replied, "What about Joseph's copper friend?"

Bill replied, "Interesting, but if there are drugs with Amy in the apartment, she might be arrested. There were a lot of bricks on the table. Also, we'd have to time this perfectly to ensure Amy's out of the apartment before shithead returns. Lastly, can we trust Joseph's copper friend?"

Tommy responded, "I agree. Could you get Natalie's help and have Amy go and stay with her at the hotel? Perhaps a weekend for the girls."

Bill responded, "That could work, but it means Natalie would know the plan. I'm not sure we want her involved. Also, I'm not sure she's got any idea how deep Amy's in this."

Tommy looked at Bill. "What about Michelle luring Amy out for the evening? I know you don't want her involved, but it could provide the cover we need. I don't see a better option."

Bill replied, "I hear you, but it's the same problem as Natalie. It's getting both involved in something they shouldn't be."

Tommy said, "Just throwing out suggestions."

Bill said, "I know, which is always helpful. With that said, I'm not prepared to involve them. Let's head up. I'll call Joseph to see if this idiot is still being discharged on Friday."

Tommy nodded as they got up from the table and headed toward the elevators. When they got upstairs, Bill went into his room to get changed. When Bill came back out to the living room, Tommy was watching the evening news.

Tommy said, "Hearing this? Looking for a man posing as a police officer on the UT campus."

Bill replied, "Did they show a picture of him?"

Tommy nodded. "Posted a sketch. It's Seamus. The report said he's got a female partner; one believed to be a student. That sketch wasn't as good, so I couldn't tell if it was Amy."

Bill responded, "This just got a whole lot more complicated."

Tommy smiled. "Only we can find this kind of trouble."

Bill chuckled. "Got that right. I'm heading in to get some sleep. Perhaps a good night's sleep will put this more into focus."

Bill headed to the bedroom.

Tommy said, "Night, Skipper."

Bill nodded, closing the door behind him.

While Bill lay in bed, his head was racing with all the things that could go wrong. Slowly, he began to think of Michelle, as well as why he was there—*To protect his daughter, no matter what.*

Bill thought of the first couple of visits Michelle made to Galveston, reminiscing about the fun they had getting to know each other. With those fun thoughts in his head, Bill was fast asleep with those great memories.

Chapter 13
November 2024

Bill woke up the next morning to his phone ringing. While Bill hoped it was Joseph with news confirming Seamus's release, instead, it was Michelle.

Michelle said, "Morning, Dad. Did I wake you?"

Bill responded, "Not really. Why are you calling so early?"

Michelle said, "Dad, the police were here. They were searching Amy's quad."

Bill responded, "What are they looking for?"

Michelle responded, "Drugs, I think. They asked if Amy's involved with dealing drugs."

Bill responded, "They're not arresting you, are they? You didn't have anything to do with Amy in that regard. Right?"

Michelle, offended by the question, said, "Dad, I've never been involved with that. Amy's been spending a lot of time off campus, but I don't know where or with whom."

Bill said, "Okay, honey. Do you need me to come over?"

Michelle replied, "The police left me alone after answering their questions. They didn't find anything in her room, nor any of the other rooms in the quad. They left just before I called."

Bill responded, "Good."

Michelle asked, "Dad, what do you think Amy's involved with?"

Bill lied, "I don't know, but it doesn't sound good. Let's deal with this one step at a time. Have you reached out to her about the police?"

Michelle said, "Yes. I texted her, but she hasn't responded."

Bill said, "Honey, stop texting her. Don't want the police accusing you of warning her." Bill said this knowing what he'd seen the night before, but he wasn't sharing that with Michelle either.

Michelle took a moment, then awkwardly replied, "Okay, can you reach out to her? I'm sure Natalie would appreciate that."

Bill said, "Let me talk to Natalie first."

Michelle said, "Okay. Dad, when am I going to see you today? You mentioned last night you had business to attend to."

Bill replied, "Not sure yet. I'll call you when we're done."

Michelle said, "Okay. Love you."

Bill responded, "Love you too."

Then Bill hung up the phone. Now that Bill was up, he figured it was time to call Joseph.

Joseph picked up on the first ring, "Was wondering when I'd hear from you!"

Bill replied, "Been working on a plan, but we've got a complication to work out. On track for Friday? You know, last night, they had a sketch of him on the local news looking for a drug dealer. The sketch looked like your guy."

Joseph was quiet for a moment, "What else?"

Bill replied, "Said he's working with a female student."

Joseph quickly shot back, "So when are you doing this?"

Bill responded, "Soon. Once the complications worked out."

Joseph got angry with Bill's evasiveness, but Bill doesn't care. After the last few interactions, Bill was concerned about how Joseph was handling this, coupled with his impatience to get this done.

The other thing Bill noticed was each of the last three times they spoke. Bill heard a click about 15 seconds after Joseph picked up. Without saying it, Bill wondered if either Joseph was under surveillance or, worse, making a deal for himself. Perhaps Seamus was his patsy, which is why Bill was being short and non-committal with details. Bill felt like he didn't have the whole story.

After a few more jabs from Joseph, because Bill was vague about his plans, Joseph angrily hung up. Honestly, Bill wasn't in the mood, as they had one day left to recon, as well as figure out the complication with Amy. Bill decided he needed Natalie's help with the situation.

Bill rang Natalie. She answered on the second ring, "Hey, sweetheart, how are you? I miss you. It's so quiet without you here."

Bill replied, "Hey, miss you too. Look, I've got a situation here. However, I can't talk about it over the phone. Can you come to Austin today? It's got something to do with both girls, but I can't go into it over the phone."

Natalie said, "What's wrong with Amy now?"

Bill responded, "It's serious. I need your help. Can you come up here, please?"

Natalie reluctantly said, "Yes. I'll be up in four hours. Text me where you're staying."

Bill replied, "Thanks, I love you."

Natalie paused for a moment, "That's the first time you've said that to me. I love you, too, have since our first date. I'll see you in a couple of hours."

Bill replied, "Great, see you soon. Safe travels."

Bill hung up. As Bill emerged from the bedroom, Tommy walked into the kitchen in his underwear, looking over at Bill and acknowledging Bill.

Tommy said, "Just put coffee on. Heard from Joseph?"

Bill responded, "Spoke to him this morning. I mentioned the complication, and instead of letting us deal with it, he flipped out. All I got was that our friend was being released on Friday. We've got another day of recon. Also, I decided to get help from Natalie. She's on her way up."

Tommy smiled, "Heard. Finally, told her you love her. Sweetening her up to help?"

Bill glanced over wryly but didn't say a word. He grabbed a cup of coffee and sat on the couch, turning on the news. It was the same reporting as the night before.

Tommy went to the bathroom, then poured himself a cup of coffee, and joined Bill on the couch.

Tommy asked, "So, what's the plan?"

Bill looked at him and said, "We're going to use Natalie as the diversion. I'm thinking we book another room for the girls—a women's weekend, where we're just visiting. Natalie can bring the girls here while we take care of business."

Tommy nodded but then asked, "I've got to ask—how much did you share with Joseph?"

Bill replied, "Nothing. I've been hearing a click on the phone line during our last three calls—about 15 seconds after we're connected. Maybe I'm paranoid, but there's a part of me that feels like we're being set up. Or maybe this has nothing to do with the Colombians at all. What if Joseph's dealing with the Feds?"

Tommy replied, "Those thoughts have entered my mind. First was his insistence on the location. Why would he involve himself that way?"

Bill nodded, "There's a lot that doesn't add up. Either way, we need to deal with Seamus."

Tommy replied, "Copy that. I'm jumping in the shower."

Bill nodded as Tommy left the room, while Bill thought about how he was going to break this to Natalie. When Tommy finished in the shower, Bill got in for his shower. By the time they got situated, it was 10:00.

Natalie texted, "About an hour away."

Bill said to Tommy, "Natalie will be here in an hour. Do you want breakfast?"

Tommy replied, "Sure, let's head down."

They went downstairs to the hotel restaurant, which was still serving, so both sat down, ordering breakfast. What was funny was that they ordered the same thing: black coffee, large apple juice, two eggs over easy, a rash of bacon, a side order of sausage, sourdough toast, and roasted potatoes.

It was funny because after Bill had ordered it, Tommy looked at her and said, "Make it two."

The waitress poured them coffee, leaving the pot on the table, while they sat quietly waiting for the food. There wasn't much to say; it was the calm before the storm. About 15 minutes later, the waitress brought the food to the table. After finishing, Bill had the waitress put the bill on his tab.

Tommy asked, "What's next?"

Bill replied, "We'll wait for Natalie. She's 15 minutes out. Once she gets here, we'll take her upstairs and explain what we need her to do. I'll also ask her to have Michelle come over so they're together. Natalie's here for Amy's intervention, and we're here to help."

Tommy said, "It's simple but effective. Do you think Natalie will go along with it?"

Bill said, "I hope so. She and Amy don't have the best relationship, but this is about Amy's safety. I've got to believe she'd step up under these circumstances."

Tommy nodded.

Bill's phone rang. It was Natalie. He answered, "Hey, here?"

Natalie replied, "Walking through the lobby right now. Where are you?"

Bill replied, "In the restaurant, just finished breakfast. We'll meet you by the elevators."

Natalie replied, "Okay, I see you."

The men walk over to Natalie, where Bill reached over to give her a small kiss. However, Natalie planted a romantic kiss that Bill wasn't expecting, especially in public.

When she was done, Natalie said, "That's for saying it first."

Bill smiled as they headed to the elevator.

Upon arriving in the room, Natalie asked, "So, fellas, what's got me up here? Why couldn't this be done over the phone?"

Tommy looked at Bill, giving him a look essentially saying, "It's your show, Skipper. Good luck."

Bill said, "I think Amy's involved with a drug dealer. How deep, I don't know. We've got a way to remove her from the situation. What we need is a diversion while we take care of this."

Natalie looked shocked, awkwardly saying, "I can't believe this. She's not even here for a year, and she's mixed up in drugs."

Bill chimed in, "Natalie, focus. We've got a way to remove her from the situation and neutralize the threat. Suffice it to say, you'll be here as cover with the girls. I need you to focus on that, please. This bantering about Amy isn't helpful right now."

Figuring Bill was about to get his head blown off by Natalie, she sat calmly for a minute.

Natalie said, "I hate it when you're right. So, what's the plan?"

Bill thought he dodged that bullet. Natalie, for all her faults, had a good head on her shoulders under pressure.

Bill replied, "Reach out to the girls. Tell them you came up to surprise them for a girl's weekend. I'm hoping that because you're here, it'll have them hang out here. It gets her away from the apartment where she's been staying."

Natalie looked at Bill, asking the fateful question, "If I'm here with them, what are you two going to be doing?"

At this point, Tommy got up and walked into his bedroom.

As he shut the door, Bill said, "Trust me, it's best you don't know."

Natalie coldly responded, "What does that mean?"

Bill replied, "I need you to trust me. I'll tell you the whole story, but not until it's over."

Natalie said, "Okay. I'm holding you to that. You're protecting our girls, right?"

Bill smiled, "Always. Text them to get the ball rolling. You're going to be here through Saturday. You wondered if they'd like to have a girls' weekend at the hotel, spa treatment, the works. Tell them you'd like to start tonight. Also, ask Michelle to come and pick out some sights and plan an outing."

Natalie texted the girls.

Natalie said, "Amy's shocked I'm in Austin, but said she's in. Michelle's a yes, too."

Bill said, "Make sure to stay together the entire time."

Without saying a word, she nodded, beginning to get situated in the bedroom. Bill walked over to Tommy's bedroom door.

After Bill knocked, Tommy came to the door, "We got a plan?"

Bill replied, "Yep, let's go finish the recon."

Tommy nodded, and then both headed toward the door. Natalie had gone into the bedroom to lie down. Tommy and Bill left, being gone for three hours doing a final recon.

Chapter 14
November 2024

During their recon on Thursday afternoon, Joseph called to confirm Seamus was being released Friday morning.

Joseph said to Bill, "You should be handling this at the hospital."

Bill replied, "I got a game plan. I'll inform you when it's executed."

Joseph wasn't happy with Bill's response, saying, "Get this done."

Bill didn't respond, as he heard the clicking in the background, so instead, Bill hung up on Joseph.

Tommy looked at Bill, "Same shit, different day?"

Bill looked over at Tommy but said nothing as he heard the whole conversation. Bill was going to get this done without sharing the details. Bill was increasingly alarmed by the clicking, not caring what Joseph thought. Bill's protecting his daughter. When it comes to her, Joseph meant nothing.

Tommy and Bill got back to the hotel at 18:00. When the boys walked in, Natalie was watching TV with the girls, which was a surprise.

When Bill got up to Natalie, "I thought this girl's thing was kicking off tomorrow?"

Natalie smiled, "Well, we decided to start tonight. Two days at the spa are better than one."

Bill asked, "Did you want to go out to dinner?"

Natalie looked at Bill, winking, "Nope. Ordered in. You two are staying next door. Got you a room so we'd have this to ourselves. I worked it out downstairs."

Bill said, "Sure. Okay, have a good night."

With that, Tommy and Bill went to their new room, where Natalie had moved their things. The boys headed downstairs to the bistro for dinner after a quick clean-up. The conversation at dinner was light, no different than any other mission. When they wrapped up dinner, it was 21:00 as they headed upstairs for the night.

When Bill got to his room, he texted Natalie, "Hope the evening's going well. I'll text you tomorrow when we're done. Love you."

Natalie responded almost immediately, "Love you too. Can't wait to hear this story."

With the texting over, Bill laid down on the bed, surprised he was asleep quite quickly, awake the next morning at 05:00. Tommy and Bill were going to leave the hotel early to stake out the hospital to see when Seamus left. The plan was to let him back into his apartment, get situated, then take him out. When Bill came out into the living room, Tommy was awake, on the phone with Amanda.

Bill whispered, "Everything okay?"

Tommy nodded, continuing to talk with Amanda.

Tommy wrapped up the call, "I'll look at it when I'm home. It can wait until Sunday. Love you too!"

When Tommy hung up, Bill asked, "Everything okay?"

Tommy stood up, "Yep. Nothing of consequence. When did you want to head out?"

Bill replied, "Soon."

Bill went into the bedroom to get changed while Tommy did the same. Within 15 minutes, they were out the door, heading to the garage for the truck. It was 06:00 when they left the hotel, but not before stopping at a Starbucks for coffee.

At 07:00, they were at the hospital waiting for Seamus's release. Bill dropped Tommy at the front door of the hospital to stake out the lobby, where Tommy sat in an obscure location, out of sight of the main corridor.

At 08:35, Tommy texted, "He's coming."

Bill replied, "Okay. Get a look at the vehicle that picks him up. I'll pick you up at the front door."

Tommy followed Seamus outside, getting the vehicle's license plate picking Seamus up.

After Bill picked Tommy up, they headed out to Highway 71 toward Austin, staying three cars behind them for most of the ride. The traffic was light, so they were easy to track. As they started into Austin, near the airport, things appeared to be smooth sailing. Tommy looked back to see if they had a tail, too—fortunately, none.

They got off the highway, heading up to the 6th Street bridge, then towards the apartment. As the driver pulled up, he helped Seamus with his bag, as he appeared to be limping.

Seamus paid the driver, then headed upstairs.

Tommy said, "What's that over there?"

Bill said, "I don't see what you're seeing."

Tommy replied, "At the corner, the black car. NY Plates!"

Bill responded, "Don't know. Let's take a closer look."

As they made their way down the street, getting closer to the car, Bill recognized the driver. It was Joseph.

Bill looked at Tommy, "I can't fucking believe this. Joseph. What the hell!"

Bill pulled out his phone, ringing Joseph. Where Joseph picked up on the first ring, "Hey, Billy Boy."

Bill quickly replied, "I'm parked behind you. Why are you here?"

Joseph got angry, "You don't talk to me like that. Who the hell do you think you are?"

Bill blasted back, "I'll talk to you however I want. You've been up my ass about getting this done, wanting no part in it other than a fee. Now you're here magically the day of?"

Joseph said, "I had no choice."

Bill heard the clicking again.

Bill replied, "You know what? Get out of the car and come back here so we can talk."

Joseph hung up his phone, opened his car door, making his way back to the truck. Bill sat in the truck waiting on him.

After Joseph got into the truck, Bill said, "What do you mean you didn't have a choice?"

Joseph looked at Bill, "The Columbians said I had to be a witness, like a loyalty oath. That's the only way we're getting paid."

Bill replied, "When did that enter into this?"

Joseph said, "It happened yesterday after we spoke. I couldn't tell you over the phone."

Bill responded, "You could've said, 'Hey, I'm coming down on business, let's meet up!'"

Joseph looked at Bill with a strange look on his face, embarrassed for not considering it.

Bill looked at Joseph, "Got a weapon?"

Joseph replied, "Yeah."

Bill said, "Okay. Come with us. We'll take care of this, and then you'll get whatever proof you need. Assuming you've got a burner phone to send the proof?"

Tommy said, "You can't make this shit up!"

Joseph nodded yes. Bill pulled down near the UT campus, finding a parking spot not far from Michelle's dorm while Joseph parked his car. Then Joseph jumped back into Bill's truck.

When he got inside, Bill said, "Joseph, Tommy. We're leading this. You take the picture when I say so. Got it. You're along for the ride on this."

Joseph was a little surprised by Bill's attitude, but Bill didn't care. It's GO time, where leaders lead the way. Besides, Joseph shouldn't be here. They made their way to Seamus's apartment complex and pulled into the back lot, where Tommy scoped things out the day before. After quickly surveilling the area, Bill looked at Tommy.

Bill said, "GO time. Cover our six. We'll go up the far-right staircase."

Tommy said, "Let's go."

The three made it to the staircase, heading to the third floor. As they reached the top of the stairs, Bill heard the TV going in Seamus's apartment. The curtain was still open, so Bill peered in to see if Seamus was alone. The only sound Bill heard was the TV. After surveilling, it seemed clear Seamus was alone, or so Bill thought. Bill pulled down his mask, disconnected the Ring bell, then grabbed his lock tools, going to work on the lock. Within seconds, Bill had picked the lock, opening the door.

As Bill stepped inside, he heard the shower running. The place was a filthy mess, shit everywhere. Bill made his way through the living room, noticing the drugs in the same spot on the table.

Bill then made his way to the bathroom. Once Bill was at the bathroom door, Tommy came to the front door, protecting their six. Joseph stood behind Tommy, keeping an eye on the perimeter, with his weapon by his side. As Bill made it into the bathroom, the shower water was still going.

Suddenly, Seamus pulled back the curtain slightly to grab a towel, slapping his partner in the shower on the ass.

Seamus said, "Honey, you've got a picture-perfect ass."

However, when Seamus saw Bill, Seamus lunged at Bill while the woman screamed. Seamus shouted something in Gaelic, but Bill's long forgotten the language, so it lost any meaning. As Seamus lunged, Bill grabbed his right arm, plastering him along the bathroom wall. Seamus hit his head so hard on the tile that he cracked three tiles, now bleeding from the back of his head. As Seamus tried to move forward, Bill pistol-whipped Seamus, quickly subduing him.

After subduing Seamus, Bill looked over at the woman, "Today's your lucky day if you want it to be. Not sure why you're here, but we'll give you $1,000 for your time. Also, you didn't see a thing - right!"

At this point, the woman was trembling. Seamus was on the ground, bleeding, unconscious. The woman was Black, standing 5'6", maybe 150 pounds, looking gaunt with pimples on her face, with straight black hair, not more than 18 years old, clearly hooked on something, seeing the tracks on her arm.

Bill asked the woman, "Where's your clothes and wallet?"

She looked a little confused. Bill said, "Put some clothes on. Show me your ID."

The woman nervously nodded as urine ran down her leg, "They're on the couch. When he got here, he wanted oral sex in the shower to start, then wanted it doggy style."

Bill responded, "Terrific, please get dressed. ID?"

She walked out into the living room, startled by Tommy, attempting to come back into the bathroom, but Bill stopped her.

Bill said, "He's with me, don't be afraid. Show me your ID; then you'll be paid and on your way."

She got changed with the dexterity of a paratrooper. Within two minutes, she pulled out her ID.

She handed it to Bill, "I'm sorry, it's my first time."

Bill looked at her, taking down her information by pretending to snap a picture.

Bill looked at her, "You're a pretty girl. Why would you want this?"

She said, "My friend, Amy, told me to come over here to party, surprise Seamus after being released from the hospital. We were looking to have some fun."

Bill replied, "See the man outside the door. He's got your money. I hope this will be a lesson. Don't say anymore. Just go before we change our minds."

Bill said this to scare her, as well as to have her make a quick exit out.

Bill called out to Joseph, "Pay her $1,000, make sure she grabs the first available cab. Then come back up here."

The woman left with Joseph. Joseph took her downstairs, hailed her a cab, and returned upstairs to Seamus' apartment while Tommy watched from the open door. While Joseph was downstairs dealing with the girl, Bill dragged Seamus out into the living room.

What Tommy saw from a distance was it appeared Joseph knew the woman from the shower. He hugged her before she got into the cab. Come to think of it, it was like the cab was waiting for her before she ever got downstairs.

Tommy went inside the apartment, where his curiosity got the better of him. He opened one of the packages on the table, slit it open with his knife, and dabbed his finger into the powder.

Tommy said, "Yep, heroin."

Bill replied, "Not surprised, are you? Given what this whole family's been into?"

Tommy rolled his eyes, then motioned toward Seamus as Seamus was coming around after being pistol-whipped in the bathroom.

As he came around, Seamus asked, "Who the fuck are you? What do you want?"

Bill didn't reply, not one word. Neither did Tommy. Joseph was back at the door where he couldn't be seen.

Bill walked over to Seamus, "Today, you meet your maker. We're here to see you enjoy the trip."

Bill took out his weapon and placed the silencer on it, resting it against Seamus' temple. Seamus began to tremble as Bill thought how fitting, a suicide. Sweat poured off Seamus, and urine soaked the carpet where he knelt. Bill could tell Tommy was getting impatient for this to be over with.

Bill looked at Tommy, "Suicide, what a shame?"

Tommy laughed as if this was a funny turn of events, "Yep, sure is a shame."

Joseph stood at the front door, looking like a cat on a hot tin roof. For someone who's been around this all his life, he was too anxious, not dealing with the situation well.

Bill asked Joseph, "What's your problem? You seem very anxious. You wonder why I'm paranoid about you being here?"

Joseph stood silent, waiting for what would happen next. Tommy was silent about what he'd seen from the balcony. He wanted confirmation or at least a chance to talk about it with Bill afterwards.

Seamus asked, "Why are you doing this?"

Bill rolled his mask up over his forehead. Seamus's eyes got wide as he saw it was Bill.

Bill finally said, "You tried to kill us on Highway 71, and you got close to my daughter. It's time to pay the piper."

Seamus said, "Mister, I don't know who you are."

Bill replied, "You're full of shit."

Tommy then said, "Let's get it over with!"

Joseph still stood silent, saying nothing.

Seamus looked at Bill, "I do recognize you. You're the bastard that killed my brother."

Bill looked down at him coldly, "I didn't kill him. I'm only here because you threatened my daughter."

At this point, Bill said to Tommy, "Go downstairs, get the horses ready to roll. I've got the rest of this."

Tommy said, "You got it."

As Tommy made his way downstairs, Bill asked Joseph to tell him when Tommy reached the truck.

When Tommy did, Joseph said, "He's starting it up now."

At this point, Bill pulled the trigger, pump—one shot to the temple. Seamus was dead.

Bill placed the gun in Seamus' dead hand, then headed to the door. Joseph went over to Seamus' body, snapping a picture, the proof he needed. Joseph and Bill made their way down the stairs.

To Bill's surprise, nobody came outside to see what had happened. The silencer made the whole excursion effective. Once they were in the truck, Tommy pulled away, dropping Joseph at his car while Tommy and Bill headed back to the hotel. Not one word was spoken.

After dropping Joseph at his car, riding back to the hotel, Tommy said, "I've got something to tell you."

Bill replied, "Go on."

Tommy said, "I think Joseph's involved in this. When he went downstairs with the 'hooker', to the cab, it seemed as if it was waiting for her. He hugged the girl before she got in the cab. Sorry, cousin or not, I wasn't expecting that."

Bill replied, "Wasn't expecting him here today either, let alone what you've shared."

Chapter 15
November 2024

As they made their way back to the hotel, cognizant of their speed, they checked for a tail and went around the hotel twice before pulling into the valet.

Before reaching the hotel, Tommy and Bill stopped both taking turns driving while the other changed clothes, then placed the mission clothes, masks, and gloves into a garbage bag. After bagging up the clothes, Bill placed them under the back bench for disposal in Galveston. Tommy would burn them when they returned.

As they made their way into the hotel, it was 14:00, so they decided to get a late lunch. When they arrived at the restaurant, the waitress sat them at the same table where they had breakfast the day before, providing them with menus and then retrieving two glasses of her best bourbons.

When she brought over the bourbons, Horse Soldier Premium Blend, she placed them in front of them, "Would you like something to eat?"

Bill replied, "Yes, I'll have the breaded chicken cutlet sandwich with tater tots. Also, can we get a side of onion rings to share?"

Tommy looked at her, "I'll have the same, please, but just one basket of onion rings."

As they waited for the food, sipping a satisfying bourbon, they took in the silence, no different than any other mission, not a lot of banter, satisfaction it's done, and no one left behind. Bill unfolded the plan in his mind, how Joseph magically showed up, sizing up what Tommy saw. Bill was a little more than paranoid.

Tommy looked at Bill, "I know that look, what?"

Bill replied, "Don't get me wrong. I wouldn't change a thing except for Joseph."

Tommy replied, "Got to say, this doesn't add up. While you were in the bathroom, he was playing with his phone. Then the thing with the girl at the cab?"

Bill responded, "What do you mean by playing on his phone?"

Tommy said, "No. He had the CNBC app open, checking the daily reports. I know what a texting app looks like."

Bill said, "I know he's family, but do you think he'd betray us?"

Tommy shrugged his shoulder with that familiar posture, "You said it, I didn't."

Finally, the food came, so they sat enjoying the meal. As they wrapped up, Bill noticed Natalie had come in, sitting at the bar. Tommy grabbed the check while Bill headed to the bar.

Bill said, "Hey, what are you doing here alone?"

Natalie turned to Bill with a great big smile, "Glad you're here."

Bill asked, "Where are the girls?"

Natalie responded, "Back to campus. Both had some things to do. Assuming everything went okay."

Bill didn't say a word, nodding affirmatively, for which she smiled at him.

Tommy walked up from behind, "Skipper, I'm heading up. I'll leave you two lovebirds to it. Dinner 18:00?"

Bill replied, "Yep."

Bill sat down with Natalie, ordering another bourbon while she drank white wine. Bill and Natalie were the only ones in the bar other than the wait staff. Natalie began to rub her foot up alongside Bill's leg.

After finishing her wine, Natalie looked at Bill, "Hey, Gunny, how about a matinee?"

Without saying a word, Bill stood up, taking her by the hand to the elevators. When they got on the elevators, they were the only passengers. When Natalie noticed this, she lunged toward Bill, starting a passionate kiss. She wore a red cotton dress and cowboy boots. She looked fabulous, offset with her dark brown hair.

While she continued to kiss him passionately, Bill reached under her dress, finding Natalie was full commando, almost like she had planned this. Bill began to finger her, and she became very excited, very quickly, having an orgasm before they made it to their floor.

When the elevator opened, they made their way to the room. As the door closed, Natalie started to pull off Bill's shirt. Bill unbuttoned her dress, and then she removed his pants. They were naked within seconds, except Natalie never took off her boots. Natalie hopped up on him, straddling his waist with her silky-smooth thighs.

Natalie whispered in his ear, "Take me inside now."

This marine didn't need more encouragement. It was 15:00 when they started a three-hour rendezvous, resulting in being late for dinner by 15 minutes.

When they got downstairs, they met up with Tommy, as well as the girls. They were seated at the table, waiting for Bill and Natalie.

As Natalie sat down, Amy asked, "Mom, you okay? You look flush."

Natalie responded, "I'm fine. I just got a little sun this afternoon."

Natalie looked at Bill, shooting him a look as if to say, "Keep your mouth shut, marine." Bill smirked, letting it be their secret. Bill thought it was hard to believe, but Natalie never asked about what happened. It never came up, even during their brief intermission. Bill thought back to the wonderful afternoon, hoping for an encore later that evening.

The dinner conversation was light, with the girls doing most of the talking. Michelle talked about a history class she found interesting, full of tidbits from this period to that period. Bill sat, taking it all in. While he wasn't particularly interested in this period of history, Bill was thrilled she was. At least the investment was being well-spent. Amy, on the other hand, clearly didn't like school.

Amy said, "College is stupid. They're just going to train you when you get there."

It was an interesting perspective. In many fields, what she's saying is true. Nobody ever throws someone to the wolves, saying, "Figure it out," it's always a team effort. There's always someone to help show you the way or work with you to figure something new out. Bill felt Amy didn't appreciate that the degree was a means to an end, building a foundation for a career. Tommy sat silently with an amused look on his face, as all his kids were grown, off the dole, having been through this with his kids long ago.

As dinner wrapped up, Bill asked, "So ladies, what's the plan for tonight?"

Amy said, "We're streaming a movie. We've not told Mom what it is; it's a surprise, especially after her surprise visit. Say, Mom, why did you come up?"

Natalie, without missing a beat, said, "I missed you both."

Bill smiled, feeling as though they dodged a bullet.

Michelle asked Bill, "Before we go up, Dad, can we have a quick chat in private?"

Bill said, "Sure."

Bill grabbed the check as everyone headed to the elevators except Michelle and Bill.

Bill asked Michelle, "Sunshine, what's up?"

Michelle replied, "Got a strange call from Mom today. She wanted to know how I was. Was I safe? It's got me worried."

Bill responded, "Well, she's your mom. That's how she rolls, no?"

Michelle responded, "I guess, but she was asking a lot of questions about Seamus, the one who tried to run us off the road. I never told her about that, did you?"

Bill looked at Michelle, a little concerned. "When I told her about Marco, I told her about what happened but only shared that someone tried to run us off the road, not the who, what, or why. Why was she asking?"

Michelle said, "Mom said she saw Seamus's picture on the news, some report on the local news, an apparent suicide at his apartment this morning."

Bill looked at her awkwardly, "I'm not following. What's this got to do with us?"

Michelle stonily looked at Bill, "The news said, 'Three men fled the scene, wearing combat gear, running toward a blue pickup truck.'"

Bill got a little annoyed, "Do you know how many blue trucks there are in Texas? About a million. What do you think has happened here?"

Michelle got visibly upset, "Dad, I know you'd do whatever it took to protect me. Nothing would be out of bounds if you thought I was in danger. I get that's who you are."

Bill replied, "Again, what's this got to do with what's happened?"

Michelle said, "I don't want you to get upset. I just want the truth."

Bill responded, "Sunshine. I told you; I'll tell you the whole story when I'm ready, not before. I'm planning on doing that soon, but I need to do it on my terms. That's our agreement."

Michelle replied, "I know, but I'm tired of waiting to know the truth. Not knowing is scaring me."

Chapter 16
November 2024

Early the next morning, Bill received a call from Joseph.

Bill answered, "Morning, what can I do for you?"

Joseph asked, "Have you seen the news?"

Bill replied, "What news? The suicide in Austin, caught it last night. Tragic."

Joseph laughed out loud, "You've got ice in your veins."

Bill responded, "What can I do for you?"

As Joseph continued to talk, Bill heard a click on the line.

Joseph said, "My associates are pleased. The package will be delivered today."

At first, Bill didn't say anything, which prompted Joseph to ask, "Billy Boy. Still there?"

Bill replied, "Yes. Sorry, I've got to run. Talk soon. Thanks for the call."

Joseph attempted to respond, but Bill hung up. The clicking on the phone increased Bill's apprehension, while Joseph seemed oblivious to it or in on it. Bill thought he had given him his chance, but he was not Uncle Jack. It was time to put some distance there. Joseph called back, but Bill sent the call directly to voicemail.

After this wonderful start to the day, Bill got up, went into the living room, turned on the TV, and then headed toward the kitchen to put on a pot of coffee. The local news came on with the same reports as the night before, except now they had conflicting reports about the color of the truck and how many were seen fleeing, even if the alleged truck was involved. Given where it was parked, in proximity to the events, it was reported that police were questioning if the two were even related.

The reporter said, "Seamus DeValera, a thirty-year-old man, was the victim of a gunshot wound to the head, pronounced dead at the scene. Police are still investigating. If you have any information, get in touch with the Austin police. Back to you at HQ."

After listening to the report, Bill turned on Squawk Box before realizing it was Saturday morning, so there were no market updates this morning. It was 07:00 when Tommy emerged from his bedroom.

When Bill saw the door opening, he said, "Coffee's on."

Tommy replied, "I smell it. Thanks, Skipper."

Tommy poured himself a cup, coming into the living room, sitting on the couch.

Tommy asked, "What's going on?"

Bill answered, "Tragic, this guy died from a gunshot wound to the head. Earlier reports about the truck, with men leaving the complex, were questionable at this point."

Tommy looked over at Bill with a wry smile but didn't say anything.

Bill asked Tommy, "When did you want to head back?"

Tommy replied, "Up to you. I can be ready in 15 minutes."

Bill nodded, getting up to head into the shower, thinking a hot shower would soothe his aching body. Bill turned on the shower, letting it run for two minutes to let the hot water come up. When Bill got in the shower, he instantly began to relax, standing in the shower for almost ten minutes, washing away the previous day.

As Bill wrapped up the shower, he had a sense of satisfaction in protecting his daughter, thankful for the friend in Tommy. As this flushed from his mind, his attention turned back to Joseph, the clicking on the phone. Bill couldn't call him, saying he heard clicking on the phone. If someone were bugging him, it'd be a clear tip-off. Perhaps Bill needed to make a surprise visit to NYC.

As Bill got dressed, Natalie came into the bedroom, "Good morning honey, sleep well?"

Bill replied, "Yeah. When did you want to head out? I'd like to be home around dinner time. Looking forward to a fire tonight, maybe a quiet dinner."

Natalie smiled, "Sounds peaceful. The girls are just waking up; perhaps we could take them to brunch and then head back."

Bill said, "Sounds like a plan."

Natalie smiled, "I'm heading back for a shower. I wish you were coming with me."

Bill smiled, "Too much company for that. Perhaps tomorrow morning."

Natalie returned with, "I'm holding you to that. We'll meet you downstairs."

Bill nodded as Natalie headed back to her room, hearing Natalie barking at the girls through the wall, updating them on the morning's itinerary, as well as it was time to get up.

Bill overheard her say to Amy, "Get moving. They're waiting on us."

Tommy and Bill headed downstairs for a coffee while waiting for the ladies. It was 08:30 when they left the room with their bags, heading to the lobby to check out before heading over to the restaurant. After getting situated at a table for five, the waiter took their coffee order.

Bill said, "We're waiting on some friends, so it'll be a while before we order."

They got the coffee at 08:45 when Bill's phone rang. It was Eva.

Bill picked up, "Eva, how's things?"

Eva replied, "I haven't heard from you. Everything okay?"

Bill replied, "It's done, she's safe, nothing more to worry about."

Eva sighed, "Thank God!"

Bill laughed, "Already did."

Eva asked, "Why the cloak and dagger?"

Bill replied, "It was necessary, but I can't explain it over the phone. After the incident, while driving home, I promised Michelle that I'd tell her the whole story but that I needed to do it on my terms."

Eva cut in, "When you say the whole story, what do you mean?"

Bill said, "Everything. I may leave out some finer points which are not relevant, but I want you to be there when I tell it. I think it's important, perhaps, to clear up some things that are either unsaid or left to interpretation. Beyond that, I won't talk about it on the phone. Can you do that for me? Come down and let me tell the story."

Tommy shot Bill a look from across the table, indicating that Bill was nuts.

Eva said, "I can if you want."

Bill told Eva, "I'll warn you, Natalie's going to be present too, as I'm doing this once, then closing these boxes forever. I know it may be awkward, but I'm pulling this bandage off once. I hope you understand."

Eva took a deep breath, "If that's how you want to do it, I can respect that."

Bill said, "Thanks. We're waiting for the girls to come down for breakfast before heading home. Let me run. We'll iron out the details over the next couple of days."

Eva replied, "Sounds good. Talk soon. Love you."

Again, Bill didn't know what to say to that. As the call wrapped up, Natalie and the girls showed up at the table. Tommy sat, shaking his head as if Bill just dropped a bomb on him.

Natalie asked, "Everything ok?"

Bill replied, "Yes."

It was 10:00 before they finally ordered breakfast. The banter around the table was light like nothing from the day before had happened. At the end of the meal, Bill paid the bill, then took the girls back to campus while Natalie checked out and headed home.

Natalie told Bill, "On my way home, I'll stop at the store for dinner. Any suggestions?"

Bill replied, "Safe trip back. I don't care. Just pick up something easy."

Natalie smiled, then headed to the elevators and down to the parking garage. Tommy and Bill loaded up the girls, taking them to campus. As they drove, Michelle noticed something hanging out of the backseat bench.

Michelle asked, "Dad, what's this?"

Bill replied, "I'm driving, and I don't know what you're looking at."

Tommy turned around to have a look. When he turned back, he had an ashen look on his face. As fate would have it, they pulled up in front of the girls' dormitory at the same time. When Bill parked, Michelle showed him what she'd found—a mask worn the day before. Apparently, one of them hadn't stuffed the backseat storage bin well, leaving it hanging halfway out.

The look on Michelle's face was one of utter disappointment. "What's this?"

Bill replied, "It's a ski mask. I've used it for hunting when it's cold."

Michelle, surprised by his response, asked, "Hunting? That's where you're going?"

Bill responded, "That's what it's for, sunshine. It was nice to see you both. I'm glad you had a nice weekend with Natalie."

Not too convinced, Michelle reached over, giving Bill a hug. "I know you were protecting me this week. I love you for that."

Bill cut her off, "Honey, I love you more than I could ever express. You'll always be safe if I'm alive. Maybe soon, I'll teach you a few tricks of the trade. Look, we've got a long trip back, so we better head out."

With that, Bill made his way to the driver's side door and got in the truck. Tommy and Bill headed toward home. While Bill was saying goodbye to Michelle, Tommy had called Amanda.

When Bill returned, Tommy said, "Just got off with Amanda. Let her know we're heading back."

Bill nodded, then set off, making their way down Highway 71. Tommy and Bill were quiet on the ride, just taking in the scenery. As they pulled up to Tommy's place, he grabbed the gear, heading for his firepit to burn the bags from Austin.

From the balcony, Bill saw Amanda waving at him. Before heading up, Tommy started the fire. When Tommy got to the top of the stairs, Amanda gave him a great big hug. Bill stayed in the driveway, obstructing the view from any pesky neighbors. Once he got a thumbs up from Tommy, Bill backed out of the driveway, heading for home.

Chapter 17
November 2024

When Bill pulled into the driveway, he noticed a car parked in front of the house. As he parked, he drew his weapon, pretending not to notice the car, mulling around in the backseat getting his bags. Bill turned toward the steps, noticing the car was empty, noting the license plate before heading upstairs, NTF 1405 – Texas Plate.

As Bill got to the top of the stairs, there was someone waiting on the deck. With his weapon drawn, Bill said, "What are you doing up there?"

A woman turned around, "Bill. It's Jenn. I had to come see you."

Bill was stunned, at first not knowing what to say.

Jenn then said, "I'm sorry for showing up unannounced, but I need to talk to you."

Bill replied, "Perhaps some notice might've been nice, a phone call. What's up?"

Jenn said, "Yesterday, I got a call from the Austin police informing me Owen's brother, Seamus, was found dead in his apartment, an apparent suicide."

Looking at Jenn surprised, Bill asked, "And you came here to tell me this because?"

Jenn said, "I'm listed as his next of kin. The police asked if I had heard from you?"

Bill looked her up and down, "What would I know about this? I saw the reports on the news about an apparent suicide. I had no idea Owen had a brother. Why would they be inquiring about me as it relates to this?"

Jenn shrugged her shoulders, "I honestly don't know. I told them we've not seen each other in years. If you were in Austin, it was a coincidence, probably visiting your daughter at UT."

Bill was suspicious, as he hadn't told Jenn about Michelle. The last time Bill saw Jenn was before Eva and Michelle confirmed it. Bill strung her out a little.

Bill asked, "You came from Montana for this? Why do you care about this guy? What's his name?"

Jenn replied, "Seamus. He was 10 or 11 when my mother and brother were killed. He was devastated when Owen left Ireland. Afterward, I had no idea what happened to him especially after going into the program."

Bill understood the nostalgia of the moment but was also indifferent to it, given what Seamus did.

As Bill pondered this, Jenn asked, "How've you been, Bill? Is everything okay?"

A little surprised by her change of direction in the conversation, Bill said, "I'm fine. I've got some news which you already seem to know. Something I didn't know the last time you were here. I've got a daughter. She's 18, and she's at UT in Austin. Eva, her mother, and I met when I was working in Nashville. Found out just after your last visit. How did you know I was visiting my daughter?"

Jenn was shocked, "Eva. Why do I remember that name? Did I ever meet her?"

Bill replied, "She came to BJ's funeral. Answer my question: how'd you know about my daughter?"

Jenn's eyes popped open wide, "The bitch who called you honey!"

Bill was instantly annoyed, "There's nothing productive to say. You didn't know her, so calling her a bitch, why?"

Jenn shot back, "She broke up our marriage! She gave you a child!"

Bill thought for a moment, trying to control his temper. Jenn saw Bill was boiling; the color of his face said it all, but he wasn't going to give her the satisfaction.

Bill finally said, "I'm sorry for your loss. Our marriage never worked because Owen lurked in the shadows long before I hooked up with Eva. You want to talk about the truth, then start there."

Bill figured Jenn would leave after that, but she didn't.

Jenn calmly said, "We both made mistakes. There's plenty of blame to go around."

Bill, wanting to diffuse the situation, asked, "Do you want coffee?"

Jenn replied, "I want to know what happened to Owen and Seamus!"

Bill turned toward the door, "Jenn, it's nice to see you. Sorry, you've come all this way for a pointless conversation that could've been had on the phone."

Before Jenn could utter another word, Natalie had just come up the stairs, stunned by what she'd been hearing.

Natalie looked at Bill, "Honey, who's this?"

Bill coldly replied, "Natalie, this is my ex-wife. Jenn."

Natalie said nothing at first, standing in shock, then turning to Jenn, staring her down.

Jenn tried to be nice and said, "Natalie, it's nice to meet you."

Natalie shook her head, "Bill, why's she here?"

Bill jumped in, "Jenn knew the man who committed suicide in Austin. She was in the area, looking for information. She's his next of kin."

Jenn picked up that Bill hadn't told Natalie his life's story yet, kindly playing along.

Jenn said, "That's right. I was down this way when I heard about Seamus. He was the friend of someone I was close to as a kid."

Natalie looked at Jenn curiously, then looked at Bill with a look like fire was going to shoot from her eye sockets at any moment.

Natalie asked Bill, "When's she leaving? We need to talk!"

Jenn could tell she'd worn out her welcome, "Was just leaving. Bill, always nice to see you."

Bill nodded, then frowned as Jenn went down the stairs, driving away. Bill turned to Natalie, attempting to console her with a hug.

Natalie turned to Bill, "You've got an ex-wife? How many wives have you had?"

Bill replied, "One. Eva and I weren't married. I promised I'll tell you the whole story soon."

Natalie hit the roof, "What! We've been getting serious, then you hit me with this."

Bill said, "Slow down. I haven't proposed but expressed my intentions."

Natalie snapped back, "Buddy, your timing's shit. Tell me when I was going to find out about her. Never!"

Bill replied, "I told you I had a story to tell. I told you I was going to tell it soon. You never noticed the pictures of the woman and the little boy in my office. You've been in their hundreds of times. You never thought to ask?"

Natalie stepped back while Bill saw her wheels turning.

Natalie then said, "I never thought I had to ask. Perhaps I should've been more curious about the man who says he loves me. Or did you say it just to get my help this week?"

Bill was trying to control himself, trying not to lose his nonsense.

Bill said, "When I said I loved you, I meant it. It's not something I say for effect. As for Jenn, my son, everything else. It'll all be told when I tell the whole story."

Natalie shouted, "Wait, you had a son too?"

Bill said, "I did. He died 20 years ago. He's the child in the picture on my desk."

Natalie was hyperventilating, "I can't believe you haven't told me. You lied to me."

Bill replied, "I was planning on telling you when this became serious. As our relationship's been becoming more serious, I knew I needed to tell you. You know some of the things from Kuwait, but there's a lot more to tell you. Look, I'd like to do this once. Can you give me the space to navigate this?"

Natalie turned to the gate, "I'm done, you lied to me. Been married to one liar already, don't need a second liar."

Bill said, "You can accuse me of omitting some things, maybe, but I've always intended to tell you the story, knowing things were getting serious between us. You might say I was choosing the best moment to tell you without burdening you. Am I making any sense?"

Natalie didn't say a word. Tears poured down her face as she turned, heading toward the gate and then to her car. She backed out of the driveway and quickly drove down the road.

At this point, even Bill wanted this over with. Tell the damn story and be done with it. Hiding it's more headache than what it's worth.

Chapter 18
November 2024

Clearly, the Saturday evening Bill planned with Natalie didn't come to fruition.

Bill texted Natalie that evening, "Are you okay?"

Bill never got a response. He sat up late, watching the glow of the lights over Galveston Bay next to a warm fire. Sometimes, when the ships are coming into port, it's kind of like its own little quiet parade.

This evening, Bill contemplated how he'd tell the story. The story itself was unbelievable as he outlined it in his own head, an ugly rendition of "This Is Your Life." Bill thought about Jenn and BJ, recalling some good times, quickly washing that from his mind. Bill felt anger when thinking of BJ's kidnapping and death, wondering again how he missed all the signs. Bill poured over BJ's death along with the subsequent few weeks afterward. At first, he felt a little guilty about the affair with Eva but then reminded himself of how bad things had gotten with Jenn. A seesaw battle played in his mind, ranging from hell yes to being disappointed for not being strong enough to stick to his commitments, essentially a breach in a matter of honor.

Bill then thought back to earlier family times spent with Uncle Jack, ballgames, days at the beach, and hunting trips—fond, cherished memories.

Bill quickly drifted back to the recent series of events with Joseph, recalling the clicking on the phone, wondering if he was being set up or if Joseph had put a target on his back. There were far more questions than answers regarding Joseph.

Bill then shifted his thoughts to Natalie; he did have the best of intentions. Who knows if she'll listen at all or forgive him? He hoped he'd get the chance. Perhaps she could accept the things he'd done to protect his men and family.

Again, all this continued to swirl in his head, and his only conclusion was that when your enemies come, they always come at what you love. Bill was becoming more entrenched in his mind; he wasn't going to apologize for protecting his loved ones against any threat. If anyone didn't like that, so be it. Bill contemplated whether to tell the story at all but had he committed himself already.

Bill didn't have remorse for Owen, Seamus, even enemy soldiers. Perhaps this was part of his marine training, being able to rationalize his actions. When in a combat situation, it's about protecting the team, neutralizing any threats, and making it back from each mission with no one left behind. Bill was willing to die for what he believed in, but he was going to take a lot of the enemy with him if it came to it. For a marine, it's pure survival instinct. Other than Tommy, would anyone understand this perspective? Bill had done terrible things for mother and country; he wasn't looking for absolution. A soldier's mission is clear: leaders lead the way, protects their team, makes sure no one's left behind and protects what you love most.

It was 23:30, so Bill headed up to bed, not before one last check of his phone. Nothing from Natalie. When he got changed, he heard his phone ping and reached over, noticing a text that wasn't from Natalie. It was an unknown number.

The message said, "Fee transferred."

Bill immediately tried to call the number but quickly got the annoying message that this phone wasn't in service. Bill tried Joseph's number, but it went straight to voicemail, where Bill didn't bother to leave a message. Instead, he turned on the TV in his bedroom, lowering the volume, hoping it would help him to sleep. Within fifteen minutes, he was out.

Bill woke up suddenly, at 02:00, to a ringing doorbell, as well as pounding on the front door. He pulled out his XDA 45ACP, slid the clip in, put a round in the chamber, and then headed downstairs.

As Bill got closer to the door, he yelled, "Who the hell's banging on the door?"

The banging stopped.

It was a woman's voice, "Bill, please let me in. I need to talk to you."

Bill slid open the curtain and saw it was Jenn, with a slight bruise on her left cheek, looking frantic.

Bill opened the door, "What happened to you?"

Jenn frantically said, "Was at the airport when two men grabbed me, held me for about an hour, questioned me about Seamus. I told them I knew nothing about him. One of the men slapped me in the face when I kept repeating the same answer."

Bill asked, "Where in the airport were you? No security was around?"

Jenn said, "No, they kept repeating I was Seamus's next of kin, so I had to know what he was into. Also, they accused me of having something to do with his death."

Bill replied, "Did you recognize either man?"

Jenn said, "It happened very fast, but I swear one looked like your cousin Joseph, just heavier than I remembered him."

Bill responded, "That's strange."

Jenn replied, "Didn't you two look a lot like each other?"

Bill replied, "Had similar characteristics. Was he a burly-looking guy, about 6' tall, with a buzz cut?"

Jenn said, "I think, but I can't be sure."

Bill changed the subject quickly, "Why did you come here?"

Jenn said, "I panicked; I didn't know where else to go. I can't afford another night in a hotel. Would you mind if I slept?"

Bill looked at her and chuckled a little, "Are you serious?"

Bill saw she was getting upset and starting to cry.

After wiping the tears away, Jenn said, "I've got nowhere else to go. Please."

"What could he do?" Bill said, "Sure. Sleep in this bedroom. I'm locking the front door, then heading upstairs for the night. Do you need anything else?"

Jenn replied, "Can I borrow a tee shirt to sleep in."

Bill responded, "Sure, like old times."

Jenn looked over at Bill with a curious smile, "Yes, honey."

Bill shook his head at her "honey" comment as he went upstairs to get Jenn a tee shirt, rummaging through the drawer and picking one out. Before he headed back downstairs, he noticed a message flash on his phone. Hoping it was Natalie, finally breaking the silence. However, it was a CNBC flash about the overseas markets, so he put the phone down and headed back downstairs.

When Bill got to the bottom of the stairs, he knocked on the bedroom door.

Jenn said, "Come in."

Bill opened the door, then handed her the tee-shirt.

Jenn said, "Thanks. I do appreciate this."

Bill replied, "Sure. I'm heading up."

Jenn replied, "Goodnight."

As Bill left, he went into the kitchen, poured four fingers of Horse Soldier bourbon, then headed upstairs for the night. He sat on the edge of the bed, sipping the wonderful premium blend, then laid down on the bed, quickly falling asleep.

Ninety minutes later, Bill was thrashing in his bed, screaming at the top of his lungs.

Bill yelled, "Take cover. Eastern flank. Incoming! FATIMA!"

Bill dreamt of the day of Fatima's mortar attack. As Bill continued to thrash around, he was awoken by the sound of his bedroom door opening. When he woke, Bill could smell the scent of bourbon in the air, with the TV playing in the background. It was Jenn, hearing him scream from downstairs. She came upstairs to check on Bill, and the opening of the door caused Bill to sit upright in the bed.

When Jenn arrived, Bill was sweating profusely, arms and legs shaking.

Jenn asked, "Bill, you okay?"

Bill replied, "Yes."

Jenn asked, "One of your night terrors?"

Bill said, "Yep."

Jenn sat close to him, "Anything I can do?"

Jenn leaned in, kissing him on the lips. Bill was a little surprised but also thought she was trying to comfort him.

After a moment, Bill pulled back a little, "What are you doing?"

Jenn replied, "This used to help years ago. Who's Fatima? Never heard that name before."

Bill smiled, "I remember how it helped back in the day. I don't know a Fatima."

This, of course, was a lie, as Bill never shared with Jenn what happened with Fatima. To be honest, this was the first time it had ever come up with Jenn.

Jenn smiled her beautiful smile, the smile like when they were first married.

Leaning in, kissing Bill again, "It's been a long time since we've been this close?"

Bill shook his head in amazement, admitting to himself that she looked terrific. Then, the images of Owen started. As all of this was running through his mind, Jenn handed him the whiskey glass.

Jenn said, "Congress doesn't take this long."

Bill replied, "What do you want me to say? You look amazing. Sure, it'll be fun, but…"

She jumped in, "Owen, right?"

Bill said, "Yes, tough images to process. How could we after all this time?"

Jenn snapped back with a cunning smile, "When there's a will, there's a way. Besides, it looks like your pal wants to come out to play."

Bill looked down, noticing he was erect as Jenn moved toward him, leaning in, undeterred.

Jenn put her hands on his face, "Can't you ever let it go? You're so busy holding onto the past, you can't see the here and now, nor how wonderful the future can be."

Bill looked at her, "What do you mean? You're saying that for one night of pleasure, I should just let it go? Do you have any remorse for what happened?"

Bill thought this would anger her, but it didn't, making her even more emboldened.

Jenn said, "Yes, I've got remorse for being weak in protecting BJ. I'm sorry. I've said it numerous times. I've beaten myself up for years over what happened. My conclusion was that it wasn't planned, nor can I bring BJ back. Don't you think I would if I could?"

Bill replied, "I don't ever remember you saying anything like that before."

As Bill's words hung in the air, Jenn kissed the left side of his neck while Bill realized he was still holding the bourbon glass, looking for a spot to put it down. After finding a spot, he placed the glass down hard, where some bourbon splashed onto his hand. Bill began to rub the bourbon into his hands to dry them off while Jenn removed her tee shirt.

Jenn said, "Don't waste it. Rub it on my breasts. I'll be tasty."

Bill was stunned. Within seconds, he obliged while she reached into his shorts, kissing him hard on the mouth. It sounds strange, but Bill was entranced in this moment.

Jenn and Bill spent a couple of hours fooling around, finishing like the old days, then watching the sunrise come up over Galveston Bay. Suffice it to say that when they were done, Bill had a whole range of thoughts running through his mind. *Was this a dream? Did this just happen?* As they lay in bed, Bill said nothing, just settling down with his head on the pillow. Jenn nestled into Bill's chest like she used to do all those years ago. Bill thought the silence was deafening.

Finally, Jenn broke the silence, "Oh honey, you still got it, even got some new moves."

Bill smiled but didn't know what to say, still in shock about the interlude. Bill continued to lay next to Jenn while she curled up even closer to him. However, this felt different as his mind wasn't racing to nostalgia. Rather, he was thinking about Natalie. If he really loved her, how could he do this? What the hell was he thinking?

Lastly, Bill wondered what Jenn's motive was for being there; something wasn't unclear. He appreciated that Jenn was frightened, but why come here looking for his help? Why now?

Chapter 19
November 2024

As day was breaking, Jenn and Bill slept for another hour. When Bill woke up, it was 08:00. He woke up like a shot, with Jenn next to him, rustling him awake gently.

Jenn said, "Bill, you're having another bad dream."

Bill sat up in bed, his heart racing, noticing he had practically ripped the sheets from the bed. Jenn was out of bed, naked, at the foot of the bed.

Bill asked, "Are you okay? I didn't hit you, did I?"

Jenn cautiously responded, "No. You thrashed around a lot, yelling for Tommy to get on his horse, Fred and Mike suppressing fire. You must've screamed it ten times. Are you okay? This is the second dream in four hours. Is that normal now?"

Bill looked over at Jenn. "I'm sorry if I scared you. No, this is a first—two in one night. Since I've retired, I've been having more of these dreams. Usually, something triggers it, but I can't figure it out for the life of me. I'll go a month without one, then have different dreams three nights in a row. None of it makes sense."

Jenn asked, "Would it help to talk about it?"

Bill deflected, "I've tried with Tommy from time to time. Amanda's told me that Tommy sleeps like a baby. He had some for a year after he returned, but they ultimately faded away."

Jenn said, "Want some breakfast? Perhaps a walk down by the beach might help?"

Bill looked surprised after last night's unexpected events, then thought breakfast would be nice.

Bill said, "Sure. It's not like we can use the bed now."

Jenn smiled, put on the tee shirt, and then headed to the kitchen. Bill got up, pulled the sheets from the bed, and got dressed himself.

Bill went into the kitchen. "K-Cups are in the top drawer. Use the Keurig now, as it's just me."

Jenn smiled. "Where are the mugs?"

As Bill headed toward the laundry room, he said, "They're in the cabinet above the machine."

Bill got to the laundry room, deciding he had enough to start a load. He grabbed the Clorox 2 and placed the sheets in the washing machine. As he poured the Clorox 2, Jenn came up from behind.

Jenn said, "Wow, look at how domesticated you are."

Bill replied, "No choice. Amanda was a good teacher—had a system for laundry."

Jenn smiled. "Didn't she have a whole routine for folding fitted sheets?"

Bill replied, "Yep, hilarious when she tried to teach me. She made it so easy, whipping the sheet around with the dexterity of a paratrooper. When I did it, it was like watching a monkey hump a football."

Jenn was all smiles, a side of her from long ago. She was still very much a beautiful woman in body, but the question was about her soul.

As Bill made his way to the laundry room door, Jenn leaned in and gave him a kiss.

Jenn said, "Can you believe last night? I've got half a mind to give this another shot."

Bill, shocked at her words, replied, "Perhaps we should slow down. I don't get how you go from last night to another shot?"

Bill instantly saw he had let the air out of her balloon.

Jenn pulled back. "I'm going to jump in the shower, then head out."

Bill replied, "Why did you come here? What were you looking for?"

Jenn replied, "I just said what I want, but you don't want any of it, do you? That's what I heard."

Bill said, "Hang on, less than 24 hours ago, we were on completely different sides of the country. You show up here asking if I had anything to do with Owen's brother. Then it's, 'Let's rekindle this.' I'm sorry, I can't connect the dots that fast."

Jenn replied, "Whatever. I knew you couldn't let it go. It felt like you did last night. You had no problem enjoying that, did you? Forget it, and I'll be out of your hair in an hour."

Rather than argue, Bill replied, "I'm heading down to the beach. Come with me. We can talk about it more."

Jenn got angry. "No, wham bam, thank you, ma'am! You're not capable of talking about it. You'll just give me the same excuses about how you'll never forget. Do you honestly think I had something to do with BJ's death?"

Bill lost it. "Are you fucking kidding me right now! You let Owen into our home. He kidnapped and killed our son. All you had to do was call me or the police and tell them an intruder was on the porch. You never had to let him in. Then you come here with some sob story about the airport, then take advantage of me after I had a terrible dream, essentially seducing me."

Jenn cut him off. "Seducing you!"

Bill shot back, "Yes. I wasn't the one who showed up with puppy-dog eyes begging for help!"

Jenn looked at Bill, asking, "You took pity on me?"

Bill shot her a look, thought for a moment, then replied, "Let's stop this. Like always with us, there's enough blame to go around."

Jenn said, "I'm sorry that's how you feel. I thought last night was a breakthrough where you'd let it all go. I was wrong. I've got nothing else to say!"

Jenn headed for the shower while Bill went outside. It was only 08:30, and already all this nonsense. He sat, looking out over Galveston Bay, watching the surf come in, figuring Jenn would soon be out of his hair.

Bill returned his thoughts to how to lay out the story, even rethinking his earlier decisions about telling it at all, strongly considering Tommy's comments—just lay it down, say nothing, move on. For Bill, it was an honor thing, wanting to be a man of his word, and he felt he needed to be honest. But how much did they really need to know, harkening back never to explain, never complain?

Before long, Jenn was outside with her purse and her bag.

Jenn said, "I've called for a car. They'll be here in a few minutes."

Bill said, "Okay."

Jenn replied, "You know, I thought I still loved you, that I wanted another shot at what we had. You can't let the past go. Do you think you'd ever forgive me, at least for closure—for yourself?"

Bill stared out over the horizon, contemplating what she said. Jenn leaned over, trying to kiss him, but he put his hands on her right shoulder to keep her away.

Bill said, "Lots to unpack there. Forgiveness? Honestly, I'm not sure. That's the best I can do right now. I'll think about it. I just don't know if I can get there."

Jenn replied, "I understand. If you do, call me. Even if you can't completely forgive, I'd like to stay in touch. I meant it when I said I was all alone."

Bill nodded. "Sure. Your car's here. Safe flight."

Jenn smiled, leaned over, and kissed him on the lips. "Thanks. We'll talk soon."

Jenn went downstairs to get into the car while Bill went with her, figuring he'd head to the beach for his walk. When they got to the bottom of the stairs, the driver was out of the car, helping her in. She waved at Bill as the driver pulled out of the driveway. Bill headed to the beach, going for a nice long walk to clear his head.

What else was coming this week?

Chapter 20
Early December 2024

It was a Monday evening, and Bill still hadn't heard from Natalie. He tried calling, but no response. It was 19:00 when Bill heard a knock on the door and pulled the curtain back to see who was at the door. It was Tommy.

When Tommy saw Bill, he said, "Skipper. Let me in."

Bill opened the door. "Is everything okay?"

Tommy replied, "Natalie's at our house, bitching up a storm. Haven't seen her this mad since her husband was banging the airline stewardess."

Bill said, "Why doesn't Amanda tell her to come here and have it out with me? I've been calling her for days."

Tommy replied, "I know. She bitched about that too, which is why I left for a walk. Suffice it to say, Amanda wasn't happy with my departure, but I don't understand what Natalie's upset about. So, you waited to tell your life story? Big deal."

Bill shook his head but said nothing at first.

Bill then asked, "Want a whiskey?"

Tommy nodded, sitting down on the living room couch. Despite the cool temps, it was a humid day, so even with a breeze, it wasn't nice to sit outside. Bill was watching a hockey game but was losing interest in it before Tommy showed up. Bill handed Tommy a whiskey.

Tommy smiled. "Thanks."

Bill replied, "Sure. Would it help if I rang Amanda? Tell her to tell Natalie to be an adult and come over here so we can have it out?"

Tommy looked at Bill. "I don't know, it couldn't hurt. I'm warning you, Natalie's wild. She's talking to Amanda about what happened last week in Austin."

Bill responded, "Amanda knew about that, so it couldn't be too much of a surprise. Also, there are only three of us who know the actual details. Natalie thinks she knows."

Tommy responded, "I know. It was funny to hear the story she spun, completely wrong, of course. Have you heard from Joseph?"

Bill replied, "No. I'm putting some distance there. Don't like how this went down."

Tommy shot back, "I know he's family, but you don't need him in your life. Speaking of Joseph, whatever happened to the payment?"

Bill replied, "Got a text from a burner. The money's been deposited. I moved it already; it'll hit my account tomorrow. I'll move your funds when it clears my account."

Tommy said, "Thanks. I wasn't asking about my cut. I wanted to see if that cheap bastard stiffed you."

Bill said, "I hate to admit it, but the thought crossed my mind. Either way, this was about Michelle. Do you think we missed anything? I've been wracking my brain. Still can't believe Joseph was there. I was so angry, I even thought about aborting, letting him deal with the fallout."

Tommy cut in, "Wouldn't have been advisable, given the car incident on the ride back from Austin. That guy got exactly what he deserved."

Bill looked over at Tommy. "Yep, easy choice."

Tommy asked, "Got a question? Why are you telling the girls the whole story? What good comes from it? Why not lay it down, move the fuck on? It's like you can't help yourself, putting your head into the lion's mouth. It's like a sick compulsion, you're never allowed to be happy. I don't get that."

Bill sat up on the couch. "I've never trusted happiness. Any period of happiness in my life has been sheared with far more unhappiness—Fatima, Jenn, Eva, now Natalie. I used to think every woman in my life was crazy. Maybe it's me. Also, how do I leave it in the past when it always seems to come back to bite me in the ass? I mean, other than us sitting here, finding out about Michelle, what good has come from my past?"

Tommy sat for a second, pondering what Bill had said.

Finally, Tommy said, "Skipper, you've got a lot of baggage. We all do. Stow it. Natalie's a great lady; she'll come around. You didn't tell me why you're telling your story."

Bill looked at Tommy. "Might be cathartic to tell it, then move on."

Tommy looked over at Bill. "Bullshit. It's only going to lead to an endless series of questions. None of them will understand. For fuck's sake, you did your duty. You did your very best in a shitty marriage. You even tried to do the right thing with Eva. Now you've got Michelle to think of. You want this story to be the legacy you leave with your only daughter? Brother, I love you, you know that, but it's time to lay it all down."

Bill smiled, looking over at Tommy. "Nice speech, but the genie's out of the bottle. I made them a promise."

Tommy replied, "Easy fix. All you've got to say is, 'I've thought about it and don't see any benefits to telling the story.' You just want to put it down. Can you call Amanda? She's texting me. Natalie's come around the track for a fourth time. I need to get home to Dodge City!"

Tommy got up and then let himself out. Bill reached for his phone and called Amanda.

Amanda answered on the first ring. "Hey, Bill. How are you?"

Bill responded, "Tommy's on his way back. Tell Natalie to be an adult, come over here, so we can have this out. She's acting like a high school girl."

Amanda paused for a minute while she mumbled over a covered phone.

Amanda said, "She'll reach out when she's ready. Also, stop calling or texting."

Bill said, "Mature. I guess another one bites the dust."

Amanda paused, then said, "You don't get it. You had ample opportunity to tell her the truth, something you never did."

Bill replied, "I planned on telling her, just wasn't sure it was serious until she came up to Austin. I just never got the chance. Also, is that seriously directed at me or suppressing fire for her?"

Amanda said, "Bullshit. Also, to answer your questions, yes. I'll talk to you later."

Before Bill could respond, Amanda hung up. Bill got angry because Amanda appeared to be taking sides, something she'd never done before.

To be honest, Bill was sick of all the drama. Perhaps he was destined to be alone. Better to be alone for the right reasons than with someone for the wrong reasons. Bill went back to the hockey game, getting angrier by the minute. Natalie was 50—stop acting like a child. Bill played things back in his head, not absolving himself of wrongdoing but rationalizing it was all due to timing. Michelle, hell, even Eva, understood his desire to tell the story once when he was ready.

If this is how Natalie was going to act when things happened, perhaps she wasn't right for him. Better still, perhaps it was a blessing.

Chapter 21
Early December 2024

A few mornings later, Bill had not heard from Natalie. Even Amanda was giving Bill the cold shoulder. It was 06:30 when Bill awoke that morning, deciding to take in the sunrise. He went downstairs for a coffee, then came back upstairs to head out onto the balcony. It was a quiet morning with a nice southeasterly breeze. The haze was coming over the horizon, while the sun would be up within the hour.

As Bill was taking in the sunrise, Michelle texted.

"Hey, Dad, I'm heading down to Galveston for the weekend. Amy said her mom is really having a hard time."

Bill replied, "Staying here or with Amy?"

Michelle replied, "With you. What's going on with you and Natalie? Amy said something happened between you guys. Did you guys break up?"

Bill responded, "Thanks for letting me know you're coming. What time should I expect you?"

Michelle texted, "Should be before noon. Perhaps we could all get something to eat."

Bill responded, "See you around noon."

Michelle responded, "Dad, are you okay?"

Bill replied, "I'm fine. Love you, see you in a few hours."

Michelle texted, "Love you too."

Bill headed for the beach, not before putting on a sweatshirt as the wind had picked up. He walked on the beach for an hour, then returned home for a shower.

After the shower, Bill made his way into the bedroom to change. After changing, he heard a noise downstairs. Reaching over to his nightstand, he grabbed his XDA 45ACP, then quietly went downstairs. When Bill got to the bottom of the stairs, he saw a shadow of someone standing at the front door. With his weapon drawn, Bill moved left, peering out the window. It was a large, burly guy, and when he turned around, Bill knew it was Joseph.

Bill opened the door. "What are you doing here?"

Joseph said, "I've been on the run since I last saw you. The Colombians."

Bill replied, "What do you mean on the run?"

Joseph said, "I've gotten myself into a real mess. I need your help."

Bill responded, "With?"

Joseph replied, "I know you were never connected, just side projects for Dad. Ones that will go to my grave. Can you look after my finances if something happens to me?"

Bill was shocked—Joseph was clearly afraid, not something Bill had seen before from Joseph.

Bill said, "Of course. Why are you on the run?"

Joseph looked at Bill, a little annoyed. "I just need financial help if something happens to me. It's best you're not involved in this any further. I was approached by the Feds, asked if I'd give up the Colombians. I'm working out a deal."

Bill looked at him like any concerned cousin. "Does that solve your problem? The cartels are ruthless. They don't just go after you."

Joseph said, "Feds told me I'm facing 30 years unless I cooperate."

Bill replied, "For what?"

Joseph responded, "Distribution, various drugs. My dad had always stayed clear of the Colombians, more afraid of them than he was of the IRA."

Bill asked, "How do you know the Feds will hold up their end? Could they be taking advantage of any discourse?"

Joseph squinted a little. "Good point, but my lawyer didn't think so."

Bill responded, "Your lawyer needs to find out exactly what they've got. But if you're going to make a deal, make sure the family is with you. They can only get to you if they're not protected. I could protect them here for a little while, but it's not a long-term solution."

Joseph looked at Bill. "You'd do that?"

Bill asked, "Joseph, anything outside of the cartel is still going to the grave, correct?"

Joseph looked surprised. "What do you take me for?"

Bill said, "You come here out of the blue, talking about a deal with the Feds. Not an unreasonable ask. What else are you offering?"

Joseph finally noticed that Bill had a weapon on him, and he became even more anxious than before.

Joseph said, "I'd never give up family."

At this point, Bill was confused. He could see Joseph was in trouble but still sensed he'd help his cousin out of respect for Uncle Jack. However, if he was wondering about Joseph's loyalty, this was the time to figure it out. Also, Bill got a feeling, Joseph maybe wired for sound.

Joseph then asked, "Do you think I'll ever talk about Owen or Seamus?"

Bill replied coldly, "I'm sorry for your troubles. I'll help protect your family if need be."

Joseph said, "Cousin, I can't believe what you're saying."

Bill walked over to Joseph, giving him a hug, but Bill was really patting him down, checking if he was wired up. Joseph noticed Bill's real intention, pushed back from Bill, and grabbed his balls.

Joseph asked, "Want to check here too? Fuck this, I'm going back to Nashville."

Bill stared at him icily. With that, Joseph turned toward the gate, heading downstairs. As he got to the car, he never looked up at Bill and then disappeared up the road.

Bill thought, *why did Joseph come here? Why's he going to Nashville?* He could've asked on the phone about taking care of his family. Something wasn't adding up. Also, if he was in the Feds' custody, how could he travel from NY to Texas and then to Nashville? Why Nashville, of all places? Bill felt like this was a setup. Joseph blurting out about Owen and Seamus didn't sit well neither did his erratic behavior.

Bill needed to talk to Tommy, as he was involved in this, too. Bill went for his walk east, walking along the shoreline for 30 minutes, then heading back toward home, past his street, down to Tommy's. This couldn't wait. Bill headed up the steps to Tommy's front door. When Bill arrived, Tommy was sitting on his deck, taking a defensive posture.

Tommy asked, "That green car gone down the street?"

Bill replied, "I don't see a green car."

Tommy responded, "Good. It sat there for 30 minutes. I noticed it when I came outside."

Bill looked at him coolly. "Joseph stopped by for a visit this morning."

Tommy looked intrigued. "Really?"

Bill replied, "Says he's in trouble. Colombians. Told me the Feds offered him a deal."

Tommy shot up from his chair. "Told you that bastard couldn't be trusted."

Bill said, "It's worse. He asked if I'd take care of his finances if something happened to him. Also, he blurted out he'd never reveal what happened to Owen or Seamus. Then he mentioned something about going to Nashville, not NY."

Bill saw Tommy's face starting to turn red, which he'd only seen 5 or 6 times over their 40+ year friendship.

Trying to collect himself, Tommy said, "He came here to tell you he's going to the Feds. He's getting his things in order."

Bill replied, "Perhaps. He said he's been on the run. I didn't believe him. Patted him down to see if he was wearing a wire, but he figured that out. It's why bolted from my house."

Tommy looked stunned. "Are you prepared to do what's necessary? This proves he'll sell anyone out to save his miserable life. I'm sorry, cousin or not, you know what this means."

Bill sat quietly for a moment, taking it all in, thinking he needed to eliminate his cousin, his own flesh and blood. Bill thought Uncle Jack must be rolling over in his grave while Bill contemplated what needed to happen.

Tommy said, "Skipper, Joseph put himself in this position."

Bill replied, "I understand what you're saying. When they come, they always come at what you love, huh?"

Tommy nodded. "Yep. Road trip!"

Bill replied, "Yes. We'll have to do some recon, then come up with a game plan."

Tommy said, "This mission will be hard. He knows us."

Bill responded, "Perhaps, but we'll deal with that once we've got a plan."

Tommy said, "I'll let Amanda know this morning. Assuming you'll tell Natalie?"

Bill replied, "Nope. Haven't heard from her. I'll let Michelle know I've got some business to attend to over the next few days, so I might not be too accessible."

Tommy replied, "Sounds like a plan, Skipper."

Bill said, "I'll call you later."

With that, Bill headed back to the beach toward home. It was 11:00, so Bill had time for a shower before Michelle arrived.

Chapter 22
Early December 2024

It was Sunday morning, 07:00. Bill went outside onto the deck with a magazine he'd bought at the grocery store. It had some interesting recipes for grilling. Michelle came out of her room early, noticing her dad was outside, and joined him.

Michelle came outside. "Morning, Dad. Sleep okay?"

Bill responded, "Morning sunshine, I did. How about you?"

Michelle replied, "Me too. Must've been all that sun yesterday afternoon, along with the drama scene at Amy's house."

Bill said, "Yep, being in the sun's a good way of getting a good night's sleep. Want breakfast?"

Michelle replied, "I can't. The reason I'm up so early, Amy texted me. She can't spend another minute with Natalie. Natalie droned on about what an ass you were, how you lied to her. Natalie said it twice when I was there. Amy said the rant got worse with each glass of wine."

Bill nodded at first but said nothing. Michelle waited for almost a minute for a response.

Michelle asked, "Dad, what's going on? You've been acting strange since Austin."

Bill calmly said, "Nothing for you to worry about. It's a long story, but Jenn came here out of the blue the day we returned from Austin. I hadn't told Natalie about Jenn or BJ despite her seeing their pictures in my office several times. I held back telling her until I knew if the relationship was serious. She thinks because I omitted things, I lied to her. I was planning on telling her and asked for the same conditions I asked of you. Unlike you, she went bananas, storming out of here, not speaking to me since. I've called her when she was at Aunt Amanda's house, asked for her to come over, but she wouldn't even get on the phone. Honestly, it's been exhausting dealing with all the drama over something this stupid."

Michelle asked, "Why didn't you tell her about Jenn or BJ? From what you've told me, you weren't happy with Jenn. BJ's death was tragic. Natalie would've understood."

At this juncture, it was decision time. Tell her the truth, or let it die a slow death. As Bill thought through his options, Michelle was getting a little impatient.

Bill finally said, "Sunshine, I don't have a good answer. Maybe I'm tired of dredging it up. Perhaps I'm afraid if she knew the truth, she'd pitch the whole thing. Telling her about you was hard enough. Having to go into all the details while we're still figuring this out."

Michelle looked at Bill. "Dad, after everything you've been through, no matter what, I will always love you. Just like the Parker McCollum song—'just burn it down'. It's eating you up inside."

Bill paused for a moment, knowing Michelle was trying to ease his burden, but that wasn't her job. She had the roles reversed. Bill also thought, *who's he kidding? What he's most scared of is the truth about Owen and Seamus coming out.* How would Michelle see him? Would she understand? He's never told her the truth, knowing the whole time she suspected more. How would she feel about the whole truth, not to mention how much of her inheritance was the direct result of these actions? Bill came back to Tommy's key question: *Was it worth it to tell this story in full?*

Michelle broke the silence. "When will you finally burn it down? If nothing else, you can tell it, be done with it. Pack it away."

Bill looked at her very cautiously. "What if you don't like what you hear? What if it changes our relationship? I've already lost one child; I couldn't bear to lose you."

Michelle looked at Bill with the tenderness of a naïve young lady. "Dad, I promise I'll understand, whatever it is. I'm sure the war was hard on you. Hell, you're still having those nightmares."

Bill replied, "Someday, I hope that's the case. What time is Amy picking you up?"

Michelle said, "30 minutes. Really, unburden yourself. I know it's hard, but it's okay to lay the sword down. Have you considered maybe writing about it? Perhaps it might help to organize it."

Bill quipped, "I'm not sure I'm ready to confess like that."

Michelle wasn't amused. "I'm going inside to pack."

Fifteen minutes later, Amy showed up, heading up the stairs like nothing was wrong.

Amy said, "Hey, Bill, Michelle, ready?"

Bill replied, "She's packing. How are you doing, honey?"

Amy said, "I'm fine. Things are much better at school. Thanks for helping me out. I know that's why you were in Austin. My mom was grateful for what you did, whatever that means."

Bill curiously asked, "What did your mom tell you?"

Amy said, "She said it was your idea about the ladies' weekend. That helped me a lot, refocused me."

Bill said, "Good, glad it helped."

Michelle emerged onto the deck. "Dad. Got to run. Love you."

Bill replied, "Sunshine, it's always good to see you. Love you too."

The girls went down the stairs, got into the car, and quickly drove off. Bill tried to look at the magazine again, but he kept mulling over the conversation with Michelle, wondering if she'd think Dad was a cold-blooded murderer. Would she see it as he does—protecting his family? Again, was it worth telling the story?

Things with Michelle were great. Bill wished Natalie would come over so they could get the fight over with, but even Natalie faded from Bill's mind. He was starting to feel indifferent about the situation.

All these things played on his mind when his phone rang. It was Eva: *Jesus, Mary, and Joseph, more drama before lunch.*

Bill picked up. "Hey. Michelle left 20 minutes ago. Everything okay?"

Eva replied, "I know, just talked to her. She told me about your conversation this morning."

Bill paused for a moment. "Really? What great insights did she have?"

Eva said, "No need to be snotty. She's worried about you. She mentioned you and Natalie are having problems. Anything worth talking about?"

Bill sternly replied, "Look, I appreciate everyone's concern, but I've got this."

Eva responded, "Look, buddy, I was trying to be a friend. Michelle's very upset, worried you'll be alone for the rest of your life."

Bill shot back, "Tell her to focus on her right now. Worrying about me isn't her job."

Eva replied, "I'm sorry, I'm trying to help. We're both concerned. You understand that. That's the only reason I'm asking."

Bill calmly said, "I get what you're saying. I'm sorry if I'm being short, but it feels like everyone in my life wants to get out of me every detail that's ever happened. You get why I don't want to talk about this, let alone burden my daughter with it."

Eva asked, "Is this about your military service?"

Bill said, "No, not by a long shot. I'm not afraid to talk about that, but there's a whole lot no one knows. Some of its hardcore, hard to tell. I'm sure it's going to be even harder to hear, harder yet to forgive. You know, there's no upside to me telling the story. Absolutely none!"

Eva sat quietly for a moment. "It's up to you to tell the story or not. You're the one who promised to tell the story once whenr this was over. Look, war is hell. I learned that from Angel. Even lived in its aftermath."

Bill replied, "There's more to this than my military service. A lot more."

Eva then asked, "Maybe it's time to lay it down?"

Bill sat silent for almost a minute, thinking, *Now I've got Tommy, Amanda, my daughter, and ex-lover telling me to lay it down. They don't get it.*

Bill responded, "Let me ask you this: Hypothetically if I said I was involved with delivering someone to a group of Mexican drug dealers, leading to a no-good motherfucker who deserved to die for what he did, what would you think?"

Eva paused for what seemed like an eternity, wondering if this was the moment Bill would finally tell her the story.

Eva then said, "I would need more context. If you were avenging the death of a child or it was to protect a family member, I'd understand. Your hypothetical question seems more specific."

Bill cut her off. "Eva, I'm sorry, but someone pulled into my driveway. Thanks for reaching out. It's always good to hear from you."

Eva replied, "Same old Bill, cut you off in a nano-second when he doesn't want to talk. Love you."

Bill hung up the phone, refusing to get drawn into telling the story and having other things to prepare for.

Chapter 23
Early December 2024

Bill made travel plans, destination Nashville, TN. He purchased tickets for an NFL game, establishing an alibi for the trip. On the ride up, Bill and Tommy stopped in Tuscaloosa, spending the night. When they reached Nashville, they were staying at the same hotel Bill used to stay at with Eva. It was strange being back; it was Bill's first trip back to Nashville.

As they got to the outskirts of town, Tommy asked, "Letting Eva know you're in town?"

Bill replied, "Think I should?"

Tommy replied, "At a minimum, it helps with an alibi. Or could it be love?"

Bill smiled. "Perhaps. Let me think about it."

Tommy dropped it while Bill considered it. They rolled into the hotel at 17:30, making good time, Bill felt. When they got inside the hotel, Bill noticed nothing had changed. The front desk, the lobby, and the courtyards were all the same.

Even one of the ladies behind the front desk said, "Welcome back, Mr. Quinn," having remembered Bill from long ago.

For some reason, when they checked in, Tommy and Bill were staying in adjacent rooms, not a two-bedroom suite. Bill didn't mind, but Tommy seemed a little annoyed with the accommodations. They got themselves checked in and then headed to the elevators. The nostalgia of the moment was pouring over Bill, remembering the wonderful times with Eva, forgetting for the moment how it all ended.

When they got to the room, Tommy said, "Skipper, I'm ordering room service, making it an early night. Since you know the area, I'll let you do some of the preliminary recon."

Bill asked, "You okay?"

Tommy replied, "Yep, just wiped from the long drive."

Bill said, "Okay. I'll see you for breakfast. 07:00."

Tommy nodded, closing the door behind him, while Bill went inside his room, thinking it was strange, but hey, if he's tired, so be it. Bill texted Michelle, but she didn't respond. Then, he thought about calling Eva. Maybe Tommy had a point, so Bill called Eva.

Eva picked up on the first ring. "Hey, what do I owe the pleasure? We didn't leave things well after our call."

Bill responded, "Uhm, I'm in Nashville. I wanted to know if you'd like to go to dinner. Tommy's here but tired; he's going to hang here. Sorry it's last minute, but I thought I'd take a shot."

Eva sounded excited. "Sure. Where are you? I'll pick you up. There's a new place I've been wanting to try."

Bill replied, "You're not going to believe it, but we're staying at our hotel."

Eva laughed. "That's funny. I'll meet you by the front door at 6:30?"

Bill said, "18:30 it is."

Eva said, "Thanks for calling. It'll be great to catch up."

Bill replied, "See you soon."

Then Eva hung up. Bill called Michelle to see if she'd just missed the text. When Bill rang her, she picked up on the first ring.

Michelle said, "Hey, Dad. Just saw your text. What's going on?"

Bill replied, "Not much. Took a road trip with Uncle Tommy. I'm in Nashville."

Michelle sounded instantly excited, "Did you call mom? I know she'd love to see you."

Bill cautiously said, "I did. We're going to grab dinner. That was part of the reason I called. First, I wanted to let you know where I was, and second, I thought to call your mom."

Michelle continued with her excitement, "So where are you going for dinner, someplace nice."

Bill replied, "Michelle, it's just dinner. We're not doing espionage. What are you doing?"

Michelle, sounding a little more balanced, "I know it's only dinner, but a year ago, I never thought you two would speak to each other again. I'm studying for a final."

Bill said, "I'll let you go so you can study. Get some sleep too; good luck on the final."

Michelle sarcastically said, "Enjoy dinner out. You crazy kids don't do anything you used to do. Love you."

Bill laughed, replying, "Love you too."

Then Bill hung up the phone. It was 18:15, so Bill hit his head, combed his hair, then headed downstairs. Before leaving, Bill knocked on Tommy's door.

Tommy answered, "Who is it?"

Bill said, "Me, dropping one of the keys to the truck. I'm grabbing dinner with Eva since you stood me up."

Tommy opened the door with a sly-looking smile, "You dog!"

Bill glared at him, "Yep, your suggestion, alibi."

Tommy just grinned, "Yeah, right. Knock her dead Skipper."

Bill shook his head as he headed toward the elevators, down to the lobby, then out the front door. Eva was already waiting in the carport, waving to get his attention. Bill started toward the passenger side, but she jumped out of the car before he could get to the front of her car.

Coming up to Bill, "It's so great to see you. I want you to drive like old times."

A little surprised, Bill said, "If that's what you want?"

When Bill got in the vehicle, he adjusted the driver's seat and mirrors before pulling out. He noticed her dashboard panel, where she had just gotten a call from Michelle, not two minutes before he headed downstairs.

Bill smirked. "Have you heard from Michelle today?"

Eva replied, "No, not today."

Bill laughed out loud. "Look at your dashboard. Want to try again?"

Eva put her hands over her mouth, laughing, but didn't say anything.

As they drove to the exit, Bill inquired, "Where is this place?"

Eva replied, "Houston Street. I plugged it into the GPS."

Bill said, "Got it."

As Bill pulled out of the hotel parking lot, he noticed Eva placed her left hand over his right hand, where Bill had it resting on the gear shift. When Bill stopped at the light, he looked at Eva, then down toward her hand on his.

Bill asked, "Fond memories or force of habit?"

Eva said, "Whatever you want it to be."

Whatever he wanted it to be, really. What's he doing here? She's already doing the full-frontal assault. He thought she made it clear in Galveston what she wanted, then turned it into some jealous rage. Bill noticed she looked terrific, having made an effort with her hair and makeup.

Eva squeezed Bill's hand, asking, "This isn't a problem. I can tell you've got a lot on your mind."

Bill played it close to the vest. "Not sure what to say. Hey, isn't that the restaurant?"

Eva smiled. "Saved by the bell, but this conversation's not over by a long shot."

Bill shook his head as they pulled into a parking spot. As he parked, Eva pulled him close, kissing him on the mouth.

Bill pulled back for a second. "Friends do that?"

Eva looked at Bill, very much like when they first were together—confident she'd get her own way.

Eva said, "I know you don't want to hear this, but I love you. I know you still love me. I've always loved you. I'm going to make it as rough as I can for you not to give us another shot."

Bill was a little shocked at Eva's aggressiveness, not sure what to say.

Bill deflected, "Did you want to eat?"

Eva said, "Sure. You might need your strength for later."

Bill was amazed; it was like old times. When they entered the restaurant, Bill thought of Uncle Jack's famous statement to him: "Billy boy, only you can find trouble like this."

Eva made the reservations but never seemed to mention it to him.

The maître d' said, "Mr. and Mrs. Quinn, this way please."

Eva shot Bill a smug smile like nothing was amiss. They got to the table and then thanked the waiter.

As they looked at the menus, Eva asked, "Do you want to get a bottle of wine? We may have something to celebrate."

Bill peered over his glasses. "I'm fine with a bottle of wine. Red. I was planning on having a steak. As for celebrating, what are we celebrating? Did I miss something?"

Eva sat with a smug smile on her face but didn't say anything. She looked amazing in the candlelight, clearly pulling out all the stops. Her hair was perfect, her perfume intoxicating.

The waiter came to the table, where they ordered the bottle of red wine along with an appetizer—fried calamari with marinara gravy. The waiter returned moments later, opening the bottle of wine and pouring for them both.

After the waiter left, Bill said, "Sláinte."

Eva said, "Sláinte, I remember, cheers in Gaelic, right?"

Bill responded, "Yep. So, how do you feel Michelle's progressing? I'm pleased."

Eva coyly said, "Changing to a safe subject?"

Equally coy, Bill replied, "We're in a public place."

Eva responded, "Doesn't matter anymore. We're free to do whatever we want."

Bill had looked over the entrees when he peered over his glasses.

Bill said, "It's an interesting perspective you have. Perhaps there's some truth in it?"

Eva said, "Do you ever see a time when you can just let the past go? I'm not trying to dredge it up all again, but it feels like you carry the past like this heavy boulder you can't get rid of. I'm amazed at what you've done for Michelle—paying for school, unleashing the huge burden."

Bill sensed Eva was buttering him up, but he played along for the moment.

Bill said, "I'm the Conway Twitty song, 'that's my job, that's what I do. Everything I do is because of you, to keep you safe with me. That's my job, you see.' She's our future."

Eva started to cry, happy tears.

Bill continued, "For me, it's an investment in her future. Say what you will about my dad, but he made sure we came out of school debt-free, so we'd start a life of our own unburdened with debt. I wish I'd done some things differently, perhaps listened more, and been more patient. If I had, perhaps I would've found a relationship with him at the end of his life. As it was, I was closer to Uncle Jack than I ever was to my own father."

Eva chuckled, "I've got to say this. Otherwise, I'll bust. Am I hearing the old marine warhorse putting things into perspective? Hallelujah, never thought I'd see the day."

Bill sat quietly for nearly a minute, making Eva nervous.

Eva said, "Honey, I was joking. Did I push it too far?"

Bill smiled. "Perhaps I'm finally growing up. I'm not mad, but I'm more confused about where this is going."

Eva asked, "What do you mean?"

Bill said, "This, us, where's it all going? I'm not talking about tonight—long-term. You've clearly outlined another plan. Share with me your grand plan."

Eva levitated out of the chair. "You really want to talk about it?"

Bill smirked. "Lay it on me, sunshine. You're a woman with a grand plan."

At this time, the waiter had come to the table with the calamari.

Bill said, "Thanks."

The waiter took their main course order and then disappeared. Both took a little of the appetizer. For Nashville, the calamari was fresh, the gravy wasn't like NY, it was okay.

As Eva wrapped up her first bite, she asked, "You want to do this here?"

Bill laughed. "You tried to swallow my tonsils in the parking lot. You've been running your foot up my leg under the table since we sat down. Suddenly, you're shy?"

Eva laughed out loud, so much that others in the restaurant noticed.

Eva said, "I'm sorry about the leg. I thought it was the table leg. I was nervous."

Bill shook his head. "Stop deflecting, it's your dime."

Eva said, "Okay. We eat, then go back to the hotel. The sex was always terrific, so I can only imagine how it will be now. Tomorrow, you head off with nothing but me in your head. When you get back to Galveston, you'll call to set up time for a visit. Two weeks, this way we can get re-acclimated to being together. With me so far?"

Bill shot her a look over the top of his glasses. "Hanging on every word."

Eva shot back, "Smart ass. I refuse to let you ruin this. After two weeks, I leave. We'll miss each other so terribly that we'll make plans for recurring trips. Perhaps you come to Nashville for two weeks, or we could alternate weeks."

Bill replied, "Okay. So, two-week trips to one another."

Eva smiled. "No, by week ten, we'll be married."

The dinners arrived. As the waiter placed the plates, they both said, "Thanks."

Bill cut into his steak, a perfect medium rare. Eva ordered a seafood dish. They each shared a piece with one another. Eva's dish was nice, but Bill's steak was better, he thought.

Eva asked, "So, what do you think so far?"

Bill replied, "Interesting, but not to be Debbie Downer. Is there anywhere in the plan for us to address specific questions? Like the last time you were in Galveston?"

Eva looked deflated. "Oh please, can we not dredge that up? I don't want to do that. Look, I'm sure we've both got questions, but can't we deal with them in the moment? Honestly, I don't want to ruin this moment."

Eva's last statement seemed to balance out the conversation.

Eva continued, "If we both get a chance to ask questions and we're honest, then it'll be fine. And don't you say it? I know what you're thinking."

Bill smiled, going back to eating his steak. Bill knew Eva wasn't going to bury her head in the sand. She just didn't want it to define their future. Again, back to her last trip to Galveston, they both needed to try to put the past behind them.

Before long, they finished supper. Bill paid the bill. Then they headed to the car.

As Bill started the car, Eva put her right hand on the left side of his face, pulling him close and planting a huge kiss on him. A kiss that felt like she was sucking the fillings from his teeth.

When Eva finished, she said, "Take me home. It's our time, finally."

Bill nodded as he pulled out of the parking lot, heading back to the hotel.

Chapter 24
Early December 2024

Eva and Bill made their way back to the hotel from the restaurant. When Bill parked, he noticed it was 21:00 looking at her dashboard. From a distance, Bill saw a big, burly man standing in the lobby, pacing anxiously, wearing a black jacket with sunglasses. Bill recognized him immediately—it was Joseph. But how did he know he was here?

Bill said to Eva, "Please, don't ask any questions. Here's my room key, 607. Use the side entrance to go up to the room."

Eva asked, "What's wrong? We don't need to hide anymore."

Bill said, "See the burly guy in the lobby? That's my cousin, Joseph. If he's here, it's not good. I don't want him to see you; it's for your safety."

Eva said, "Okay, I'll head in through the side entrance."

Bill replied, "If I'm not upstairs in 30 minutes, knock on the adjacent door in the room. Tommy's sleeping in the next room. Tell him what happened."

Eva replied, "Bill, you're scaring me."

Bill said, "I don't know what's happening, but I need you to be comfortable being uncomfortable. I need to see why he's here. I'll text you when I'm coming up. Also, the safe word is OMAHA. You don't open the door unless you hear it. Got it?"

Eva started to get nervous, flush.

Bill tried to calm her. "Sunshine, focus, breathe. Focus on what I asked, repeat it to me."

Eva said, "Room 607, use the side entrance and wait for 30 minutes until you come up. You'll text when you're coming up. If I don't hear from you after 30 minutes, wake Tommy. Don't open the door unless I hear OMAHA. What do I do if I don't hear the safe word?"

Bill replied, "Here's my weapon. It's loaded. If you don't hear the safe word, empty the weapon into the door."

Eva replied, "I'm not sure I can do this!"

Bill calmly said, "My training taught me to be comfortable being uncomfortable. No emotions, no hesitations. This could be life or death. Focus and concentrate on your breathing. Stay behind the desk for added protection. Remember, when you pull the trigger, aim ¾ of the way up the door. Got it? I know it's a lot, but this is about protecting Michelle and defending us."

With his last statement, Eva stiffened up—mama bear's instinct kicking in to protect her cub. It was exactly what she needed to hear.

Bill said to Eva, "Got a plan. It's about execution now. Control your breathing. Everything's going to be fine."

Eva, with tears streaming down her face, said, "I love you. I need to hear you say it!"

Bill looked at her. "I've always loved you, not sure I ever stopped. But let's focus, execute. We can save the kisses for when it's over. Ready, go."

Before Eva could respond, Bill opened the driver's side door, making himself a diversion so she could make her way in the side door. As Bill entered the lobby, Joseph stood up, walking directly toward him. Both of Joseph's hands were at his side, as Bill quickly scanned the area to see if Joseph wasn't alone—associates or Feds. It appeared he was alone.

When Joseph reached for Bill's hand, he said, "Billy Boy. Glad to see you."

Bill responded, "Same here. How'd you know I was here?"

Joseph dismissed this, "Not important. I need some help. I'm on the run, running low on cash. Could you lend me $10,000? You know I'm good for it."

Bill shook his head. "Sure, I can float you that, but I don't carry that kind of cash on me. Anyway, I can't do that unless you answer my original question."

Joseph got angry. "Fine. You won't help me."

Bill shot back, "I'll help, but answer my question. Want to get a drink at the bar?"

Joseph looked around nervously. "Sorry. I've been going nuts lately."

Bill replied, "Let's head to the bar."

As they walked to the bar, Joseph looked as if he were stumbling a little, like he had a few cocktails before Bill arrived. Upon reaching the bar, the bartender confirmed Bill's suspicion.

The bartender said, "Hey pal, back again?"

Joseph said, "Make it two. One for my cousin."

The bartender replied, "Cousins, I see it."

Bill nodded but didn't engage, nor did Joseph.

The bartender brought over the drinks, asking Joseph, "Charge to the same room?"

Joseph nodded, then looked at Bill. "Do you know how my dad always seemed to know where you were? He used tracking devices on everyone, learned at the hand of the master."

Bill was a little annoyed. "How did you get a tracking device on me?"

Joseph replied, "Your truck in Austin."

Bill got angry. "What the fuck! You treat your own flesh and blood like this! I've got to say, I'm really pissed off."

Joseph replied, "I had to. It was for your protection."

Bill shot back, "That makes no sense; it explains how you found me but not why you're here."

Joseph said, "I've got a rat in my organization. When the Mexicans picked up Tavares, he sang like a canary before they killed him, telling them someone on the inside was talking to the Feds."

Now Bill was fit to be tied. "So, you think I'm the rat? Some cousins, you're talking to the Feds, but I'm the rat?"

Joseph calmly looked at Bill. "I made up that story so I could surveil you to prove you weren't the rat. To be honest, I never thought it was you. You had nothing to gain."

Bill shot back, "Give me a fucking break! You're covering your ass and whoever else I'm talking to. Cousin, our path ends here. No more contact, no more meetings. Got it? There's no way I'd let anyone treat me like this, especially my own flesh and blood."

Before Joseph could respond, Eva texted, "Is everything okay? It's close to 30 minutes."

Bill said to Joseph, "Sorry, I need to take this."

Joseph was slurring his words at this point. "Sure thing."

Bill texted Eva back. "So far, yes."

Then he put the phone back in his pocket.

Bill looked at Joseph. "I'm done here. Got to run."

Joseph replied, "You know, back in the day, my dad contemplated whacking you after the whole Owen thing—tie up loose ends. I talked him out of it."

Bill was stunned. Joseph just threatened him with the ultimate penalty. Bill stared coldly into Joseph's eyes, wondering if anything else needed to be said. However, Bill saw the bartender coming over with the bill.

The bartender asked, "Do you guys want anything else? It's last call."

Both shook their heads no. Bill noticed Joseph scribbling out his signature, along with his room number, 705.

As they gulped their last drop, Joseph looked at Bill. "I saved your life that day."

Bill replied, "You're full of shit. Like I said, the road ends here. It's a shame. You're the last bit of family I've got left, but with your antics, no family is worth it. Families are overrated."

Joseph icily replied, slurring his words, "Who the hell do you think you're talking to? I'm Joseph from Brooklyn, I'm known. You aren't known at all, not unless I make you known."

Bill grabbed Joseph by the shirt collar. "Come near me or my family again, they'll need dental records to identify you. Don't you ever fucking threaten me again?"

Bill left Joseph at the bar, heading to the elevator, then texting Eva – "On my way up".

When Bill got to the door, he said, "OMAHA."

Seconds later, Eva opened the door. What Bill didn't expect was Tommy was sitting with her, weapons drawn.

Tommy asked, "What was that all about? Joseph is at this hotel!"

Bill replied, "Told me he put a tracking device in my truck in Austin. Told me a few other things, too."

Eva came up to Bill, hugging him tightly, sobbing into his chest.

Tommy replied, "Such as?"

Bill said, "Apparently, the tracking device was for my protection. He mentioned something about Tavares singing like a canary. Flushed out on his side as someone else was talking out of school to the Feds. He accused me of being a rat, then dropped another bombshell— back in the day, Uncle Jack wanted me taken out to tie up loose ends. It was Joseph who stopped it. He said he saved my life; don't you know?"

Eva was now sitting on the couch, her hands over her mouth, shaking, having no knowledge of what Bill was talking about. Bill walked over to her, putting his hand out as she reached for his.

Bill looked at Eva. "It'll be okay. We need a game plan. Eva, you'll be our alibi."

Eva was stunned, not believing how cold Bill became.

Bill said to Eva, "This is about protecting us all now. Joseph made it clear tonight: he's looking out for number one. No one's safe."

Eva said, "Okay, alibi?"

Bill responded, "All you need to do is stay here, then back up the story I'm about to tell, if ever asked. We went to dinner; Tommy was waiting for us when we got back. We hung out in here the rest of the evening before heading to bed, say 23:00. That's our story."

Eva nodded but said nothing.

Tommy then asked the fateful question. "What's the plan, Skipper?"

Bill replied, "Surprise attack tonight. We've got the horses ready to go."

Tommy asked, "Is he alone, or is it a trap?"

Bill responded, "Good question. We'll need to recon the lobby, the bar, as well as the balcony. I didn't notice anyone with him. Did you bring your dip up or leave it in the truck?"

Tommy replied, "I finished one up here but left one in the truck. Why?"

Bill said, "Give me the keys. I'll go down for some night air and a dip. I'll scout the lobby and walk the courtyard to see if he's alone."

Tommy said, "Let me get the keys."

Then Tommy got up, heading into his room through the adjacent door.

When Tommy closed the door, Eva burst into tears.

Bill said, "I know you're scared, but you need to overcome that fear. I need you to trust me and follow my instructions. I'm not going to let anything happen to you or Michelle."

Eva nodded as the tears seemed to fade. Tommy entered the room, tossing Bill the key.

Tommy said, "I've got my pistol; she's got yours. What else do you need?"

Bill replied, "We'll see when I'm back. Lay out the gear. I'll be up in 30 minutes. Eva, stay here with Tommy. You'll be safe."

Eva nodded.

Tommy said, "See you in 30."

Bill put on his ball cap, headed out the door toward the elevators, and placed his weapon in his back belt. When he reached the lobby, he headed for his truck to get the Skoal. When Bill got to the truck, he went to the passenger side front door, opened it, and looked for the Skoal, but also looked for the tracking device. Bill thought about Joseph's movements in Austin—could it be on this side of the truck? Bill looked in the front seat, finding nothing, but when he went into the back seat, he felt around inside the pocket of the passenger seat. Bingo. Found one. Bill ran his hand underneath the bench to see if he had planted more than one, finding a second. Bill then inspected the driver's side—front and rear—but found no more. Lastly, Bill laid on the ground to see if anything was under the truck—no other devices.

Now Bill loaded up the Skoal in his front left cheek, instantly making the left side of his mouth go numb. He stood outside the front door, pacing as if he was trying to stay warm while doing his bad habit. Bill noticed the front lobby had two people working—a young man and a young lady, college kids if he had to guess. Both seemed more interested in each other than what was happening at the front door.

After 30 minutes of pacing, Bill headed inside, walking the courtyard, where he saw the bar was closed. From what Bill saw, nobody was scoping out the courtyard or the balconies. Bill stopped a couple of times in the courtyard to see if any windows had open shades, but none did. After his recon, Bill headed back to the room, formulating a plan.

While Bill was in the truck, he grabbed the ski caps. One thing he noticed by the front desk was they only had one camera on the ground-floor exits. Nothing on the elevators or any of the floors.

When Bill got back upstairs, Tommy and Eva were watching TV, anxiously waiting for his return. When Bill opened the door, Eva jumped into his arms with a warm but scared hug.

Bill said, "Eva, it's going to be okay."

Tommy, understanding the situation, said, "Got a plan?"

Bill said, "Yes. Security's light, but I brought the masks just in case. We'll go up the back stairs to the 7th floor, make it look like maintenance workers are there to fix a problem."

Tommy said, "What if he doesn't come to the door?"

Bill replied, "I've got my tools. You'll cover our six while I pick the lock. Joseph was drunk when I left him, so we've got that to our advantage."

Tommy nodded. "Like it."

Bill looked at Eva. "Go inside, take one of my tee shirts for something to sleep in. Tommy and I will be gone for a bit. Keep this weapon with you. Lay down in bed with the weapon under your pillow. Turn on the TV so you'll see if anyone's approaching. It's fine if you fall asleep; I don't expect anything to happen. We'll be back when we're done. Also, give me your phone. I'll text you on my phone when I'm coming back. It will be something other than we're heading back up—passcode the same, 0317?"

Eva looked at Bill handing him her phone. "Yes, the code's the same. I can't believe you remembered that. Bill, we can't lose you. You do whatever you have must to get back to us. Both of you. Safe word's the same?"

Bill nodded, replying, "Yes."

Bill didn't say anything else—there wasn't much else to say. It was GO time. All this sentimentality could come later. Tommy and Bill changed clothes. For a moment, Bill considered the aftereffects of eliminating his cousin, then quickly put that out of his mind. This was about protecting his family. As Bill headed to the stairwell door on the 6th floor, he was amazed at what had happened, as well as what was about to happen.

Chapter 25
Early December 2024

Bill made his way up to the 7th floor, stunned that a pass key wasn't needed to get onto the floor. As Bill made his way into the stairwell, he double-checked for cameras, finding no visible evidence of any. When Bill got to the top of the stairs, he opened the stairwell door, emerging onto the 7th floor. Room 705 was next to the stairwell, making for a quick exit when needed.

As Bill closed the door, he heard Tommy entering the stairwell behind him. Bill proceeded as planned. As he got to the door, Tommy entered the hallway, heading Bill's way. Tommy gave Bill a nod, all clear sign. Bill then knocked on the door. To his surprise, Joseph came to the door in a drunken haze.

Joseph asked, "Who's there?"

Bill manipulated his accent and replied, "Maintenance, we've got a gas leak."

Without missing a beat, Tommy came up behind Bill, protecting their six. Much to Bill's surprise, Joseph opened the door. As Joseph opened the door, Bill pulled down his mask, bolting into the room the minute Joseph cracked the door. When Bill pushed in the door, Bill punched Joseph in the jaw, forcing him down to the ground like a ton of bricks. Joseph was unconscious before he hit the floor. Tommy entered the door, shutting it behind him.

Bill said, "I'll secure him. Sweep and clear the bedroom."

Tommy nodded, heading toward the bathroom, then the bedroom. When he got into the bedroom, there was a young woman on the bed, slurring her words terribly, almost incoherent. The young woman was a Hispanic woman, 5'2", maybe 100 pounds, with straight brown hair and track marks on both of her arms.

Tommy said, "Hey there, time to get dressed. Party's over."

The girl then collapsed on the bed, overdosing in front of Tommy. Tommy saw fresh track marks, as well as freshly snorted powder on the woman's nose. Tommy thought she didn't look much more than 20 years old.

After securing Joseph, Bill asked Tommy, "Clear?"

Tommy replied, "We're clear now. But we've got a problem."

At this point, with Joseph unconscious as well as having his hands tied behind his back with zip ties, Bill went into the bedroom.

Bill said, "What's the problem?"

Bill hadn't seen the dead woman sprawled out on the bed, arms over her head, legs spread wide open, with her feet dangling to the floor. Bill touched her choreatic artery but she had no pulse.

Bill looked at Tommy, "It's sad, but this presents an opportunity. A prostitute and bad drug deal."

Tommy smiled at Bill, "Sometimes, Skipper, you've got one demented mind. You should be a fiction writer."

Bill didn't respond, not knowing what else to add. Bill then turned toward the bedroom door; hearing Joseph begin to moan.

Bill heard Joseph say, "What the hell happened? Why am I bleeding?"

Tommy asked Joseph, "What are you doing in here with that girl?"

Joseph, still hazy from the knot on his head, said, "I picked her up tonight. I didn't know she was with you guys. Honest, she never said anyone's putting her out."

Tommy replied, "That makes it right to OD her. In our town, isn't how roll."

Joseph was still hazy. "Look, I've got $50,000 in cash in the bedroom. Let me live and it yours."

Bill grabbed Joseph's phone on the floor, while Tommy asked, "What's the passcode?"

Joseph said, "Look, I'm leaving in the morning. I don't want trouble. Please, I've got two kids at home."

Tommy chuckled. "Should've thought of them before you pulled this stunt."

Tommy then kicked Joseph in the ribs on his right side. "Passcode."

Joseph said, "Why do you need my phone?"

Tommy kicked him again in the ribs. "Passcode. We can do this all night, or at least until I puncture your lung. Ever had a punctured lung? Real painful. Can't breathe without being in a lot of pain."

Joseph finally said, "040167."

As Tommy interrogated him, Bill made sure they had silencers on their weapons. Bill brought two weapons with him, knowing both were clean. Bill motioned to Tommy with his weapon, seeing Tommy needed to put his silencer on. Joseph sensed what was coming, moaning. Bill, after putting his silencer on, began to look at Joseph's phone, showing it to Tommy.

Bill said, "Look at that."

Tommy replied, "What am I looking at?"

Bill replied, "Tracking software. Look at the list of contacts. That's me, he's got Michelle in her too, as well as some 615 area codes." Bill reached behind Joseph, cutting the zip ties from his wrists.

Tommy, after giving Bill a moment of silence, asked, "What now?"

Bill asked Joseph, "Why are you tracking these people?"

Joseph now recognized Bill's voice, "So, cousin. I don't think you've got the stones to do this."

Bill replied, "You're not my cousin anymore. Not after this. You were involved, trying to hurt my daughter. Nobody gets away with that as long as I'm alive."

Joseph replied, "Fuck You! You haven't got the …."

Bill placed the weapon to the back of Joseph's head, then pulled the trigger. Joseph was dead instantly.

Bill looked at Tommy, then down at his cousin. He made a sign of the cross over his cousin, out of respect for Uncle Jack.

Tommy said, "We've got a move."

Bill replied, "Go into the bedroom, put this weapon in her hand, then bring her shit back in here. We'll place them so it appears as though there was a struggle, a john, a hooker. Drug deal went bad."

Tommy said, "I like where you're going."

Tommy went into the bedroom, placing the weapon in her hand, then retrieving her clothes. She was naked in the bedroom, so they could stage it as though she shot Joseph after having sex. It was clear they had sex—no missing that with the girl sprawled out on the bed.

While Tommy was in the bedroom, Bill went through Joseph's pockets, finding his wallet and car keys. When Bill opened the wallet, he found about $700 in cash along with two credit cards, but no pictures or driver's license.

When Tommy returned from the bedroom, he said, "All done. Let's wrap this up."

Bill asked Tommy, "Here's his wallet. Get her fingerprints on it, and then stuff it in her bag, but leave the bag open."

Tommy said, "Copy that."

Tommy went to the bedroom to place her fingerprints on the wallet, returning in seconds then put the wallet in her open purse.

Bill said, "Give me her purse. Spread the clothes around the room like they were tearing the clothes off before getting laid. I'll place his wallet in her handbag, leaving it open on the coffee table. They fucked; Joseph came into the living room; sees she's lifted his wallet. She comes in behind him, orders him on his knees, BANG, returns to the bedroom, does a few bumps, then ODs with the gun in her hand. Tragic, huh?"

Tommy laughed, "What the hell's wrong with your mind?"

Tommy was amazed at how quickly Bill thought to stage the scene. Bill placed the purse on the coffee table, leaving it open. Tommy didn't say a word, walking into the bedroom, putting a bag of heroin on the granite counter, and spreading some dust across the countertop. Tommy found it on the table in the hotel room.

Tommy returned to the living room. "Anything else?"

Bill replied, "Need to text Eva."

Tommy nodded. "Let's get moving, Skipper."

Bill nodded, texting Eva. "I'm in the living room. You're sound asleep. Can't believe what a wonderful evening to restart what I've so desperately wanted. I love you so much."

While Bill wrapped up the text, Tommy opened the door, scouting the area. It was 03:30, with the coast clear. They left the room, heading downstairs. When they got back, Eva was sound asleep. Tommy went to his room while Bill quietly changed in the bedroom.

After changing, Bill touched Eva on the shoulder. "We're back."

Eva smiled as she closed her eyes. Bill left the bedroom, closed the door behind him, putting on the TV in the living room. Bill was too wired to sleep, retracing the events over the past few months, weighing things in his mind. Bill grabbed an empty water bottle along with a tin of Skoal, loaded up his left cheek, and sat in front of the TV. He found an old movie that initially appealed to him, but it lost its allure just as quickly.

Bill decided to head to bed, but not before brushing his teeth. As he lay down in bed, Eva rolled over, snuggling up close. Bill couldn't believe this turn with Eva. As she nestled her head inside his shoulder, Eva began to run her fingers over Bill's chest.

Bill asked, "Awake?"

Eva said, "Not really. I want us to be this close always. Go to sleep. Is it over?"

Bill replied, "It is."

Chapter 26
Early December 2024

Bill woke up the next morning at 08:00, hearing Eva on the phone in the living room. She had closed the door to muffle the sound. Bill opened the door slowly, not making much noise. When Bill came in, she was wearing his tee shirt, her hair a little messy, and rubbing her eyes, but not appearing to be upset.

Bill whispered, "Everything okay?"

Eva nodded, then showed Bill she was talking to Michelle. Bill went back into the bedroom, laying back down, trying to close his eyes, wanting to go back to sleep, but 15 minutes later, Bill overheard Eva again.

Eva stated, "Why do you think that? Your father won't let anything happen to you unless you want it to. Believe me, I've seen the way he protects those he loves. He wouldn't permit it!"

This piqued Bill's curiosity, so he went back into the living room.

Bill whispered, "What's going on?"

Eva waved Bill off as if to say not now—she was talking Michelle off the ledge. Bill sat on the couch, where Eva came to sit with him at first. After ten minutes, Eva began to rest her head on Bill's lap, continuing the conversation with Michelle. Bill grabbed the TV remote to put the TV on. As soon as the picture came up, Bill turned the volume down low so it wouldn't interrupt their conversation.

As they continued to talk, the morning news channel came on with a breaking story.

The newscaster said, "A drug deal's gone bad in a downtown hotel. Reporting from the scene is Michael Duffy. Michael, what's happening at this popular downtown hotel?"

Michael Duffy said, "Michael Duffy reporting live, where a man and a woman were found dead in a 7th-floor suite this morning. It appears to be a drug deal gone bad, according to my source. This is an active crime scene. We'll bring you more as it unfolds. Back to the studio."

Eva wrapped the call with Michelle. "She's fine. What are you watching?"

Bill replied, "Morning news. Did you tell Michelle about last night?"

Eva said, "No. She asked, but all I said was that we had a nice dinner. Too many questions to be answered, and she'll be way too excited. She's tough on the outside but a huge romantic on the inside. Besides, we're still figuring things out."

Bill responded, "Not sure I follow."

Eva replied, "Don't get me wrong, last night was terrific up to the point we got back to the hotel. It's going to be great moving forward, but I'm not sure how she'll handle this. She told me before she left for school that she dreamt we reconciled. I'm positive she'll be happy for us but concerned as well. Am I making any sense?"

Bill said, "A little. Let's keep it to ourselves for the moment. If things work out, we'll pull it off as a surprise. I could go get her from Austin while you happen to be at the house in Galveston when we return. What do you think?"

Eva responded, "Well, that's one way. Look, let me handle this one, okay?"

Bill chuckled, "Oh, so I'm as tender as a busted chainsaw, huh?"

Eva smiled, deflecting. "What happens now? Did you want to talk about last night?"

Bill was puzzled. "What do you mean, what happens now? We can talk about anything you want. If we're going to be in a relationship, it'll be crucial that we talk from time to time. Last night was all about us, no?"

Eva smiled a great big smile, popping up to give Bill a kiss, guessing it was the response she wanted.

Eva said, "Okay. Let's start with what happened last night when you left with Tommy."

Bill became cautious with his posture, which Eva noticed.

Bill shook his head. "Let's just say I wouldn't want you to be an accessory after the fact. They came at what I loved; I'm convinced Joseph was part of reaching out to Michelle, which launched the Seamus episode. Does that make any sense?"

Eva paused for a moment. "Complete sense. This story on the news, was this the protection you're speaking of, hypothetically, of course?"

Bill took a deep breath. "Sunshine, it isn't about *was* or *wasn't*. The issue is, why did he attempt this? They said it was a drug-related death. Maybe a deal went bad; perhaps the girl was a hooker and shot him for his money and or the drugs. Why would I have anything to do with that?"

Eva looked at Bill, getting angry with his evasiveness, but he didn't care. He was protecting her too at this moment, and he wasn't going to be judged or apologetic for protecting his family?

Eva asked, "What do you mean you're protecting your family? Tommy is a close friend, not family."

Bill replied, "Tommy's the only family I've got outside of Michelle, and hopefully you. Michelle's my whole life now. Seeing how she flourishes will be our greatest achievement. When BJ's died, that was stolen. You gave that back to me, no matter how long it took. Also, if we're rekindling whatever this is, you'll be my family, too. Perhaps I jumped the gun, protecting you last night, but have you not met me before?"

Eva laughed. "But why can't you tell me what happened last evening? I knew you were going to confront your cousin."

Bill responded, "What would you like me to say? Want a blow-by-blow account? My own flesh and blood was tracking all of us. Did you know my Uncle Jack was involved with the Colonel and Angel? I mean, really, you need all the sordid details, hypothetically, of course."

Eva was upset, and Bill saw her eyes welling up with tears.

Bill said, "Sunshine if you love me like you say you do, you need to trust me. Let me assure you that ignorance is bliss right now regarding this. I've said I'll lay out the whole story someday soon. However, today's not the day."

Eva angrily replied, "You've been promising that for weeks. You'll tell us the whole story. Not sure what that even means."

Bill replied, "I am and will do it once. Get it back inside the box, then lose that box forever. I'm prefacing it with you—it's ugly, hardcore, gruesome. My worst fear is that either you or Michelle, or both, can't understand then choose to keep me out of your life. I can't say how crushing that would be."

Eva said, "Honey, when I say I love you, it means warts and all."

Bill laughed, "Can I hold you to that? I'll remind you of that after you've put your hands over your mouth a few thousand times when I tell this story."

Eva laughed out loud.

Bill asked Eva, "What's happening with Michelle? Anything to be concerned with?"

Eva laughed. "Well, she wanted to know how dinner went."

Bill smiled. "Did you tell her we weren't doing espionage?"

Eva smiled. "Like I said, I told her it was a nice dinner."

Bill asked, "So what was all the drama over this morning?"

Eva replied, "Stop that. She met a boy at school and wondered how to tell her dad. She said he was nice and polite on their first date. He's in the history department and eventually wants to be a lawyer. Patrick was his name. On the first date, all he talked about was the history class they had, as well as his love of the law. She sent me a picture; he's cute, but she said he needed to work on his small talk. I reminded her that's normal for boys his age."

Bill sighed. "Mr. Right or Mr. Right now?"

Eva smiled. "Never know. I'll say this—she's got your instincts for flushing out the frogs. She didn't spend nearly the amount of time I did kissing that many frogs."

Bill replied, "Did she provide this loser's last name?"

Eva laughed. "Typical Dad. Mc something, McTiernay, I think."

Bill developed a very ominous look; his face went ashen.

Eva asked, "Are you okay? You look like you saw a ghost."

Bill pursed his lips. "Patrick McTiernay? Did she say where he grew up? Jenn was Maura Jennifer McTiernay. Son of a bitch, she lied to me about not having children!"

Eva jumped in. "Slow down, could be a coincidence. Michelle said he's from the Pacific Northwest, maybe Montana. Also, you don't know if they're related."

Bill looked at Eva deadpanned. "I don't believe in those kinds of coincidences. Smith or Martinez, common names, maybe. McTiernay isn't a common name. When Jenn first popped up out of the woodwork, she told me she and her father had been living in Montana in the witness protection program. She gave me some bullshit about never being fortunate to remarry or have children. It's Owen all over again!"

Eva was stunned, not sure what to say, not being able to piece any of this together.

Bill paused for a moment. "I know how we can find out. I'll call Jenn."

Eva said, "What? How do you know how to get in touch with Jenn?"

Bill replied, "Jenn gave me her contact information last month when she was in Galveston. Why she was there is still a mystery."

Tommy knocked on the adjacent door. "Hey, you guys decent in there?"

Before Bill could respond, Eva said, "Yes, come in. We're just talking."

When Tommy walked in, he saw the look on Bill's face. "Something vexes thee?"

Tommy's attempt to lighten the mood wasn't appreciated by Bill. Why had Jenn re-emerged from the shadows? Was she in town to visit her son? Why had she lied about having a son? Tommy could tell a lot was weighing on Bill's mind, and so could Eva.

Tommy said, "What's wrong, Skipper?"

Bill replied, "Not sure yet. Hey, we should get moving. Not sure if you saw the news, but it's going to be murder getting out of here."

Tommy smiled. "Saw the news, tragic."

Eva chimed in, "That's all you've got to say?"

Bill responded, "It's tragic. What else is there to say?"

Eva sarcastically said, "Okay. I'm hitting the shower. Want to join me?"

Tommy smiled. "I'll leave you two alone."

Bill replied, "A raincheck, got some thinking to do."

Eva rolled her eyes, leaving for a lonely shower.

Tommy said, "I hate it when you get that look."

Tommy went back to his room. Eva had gotten in the shower, and Bill went into the bedroom to start packing up. When Eva finished her shower, she came out of the bathroom with a towel wrapped around her chest and another wrapped around her head.

Eva said, "Shower's yours, honey."

Bill replied, "Thanks."

It was 09:00, and by 09:30, they were downstairs eating breakfast.

Jenn's got a son; Bill couldn't believe it. But what did they want with his daughter?

Chapter 27
Early December 2024

When Bill got to the lobby, the police were swarming the front desk, asking each person checking out if they'd seen or knew this man or this girl. Tommy and Eva started over for breakfast while Bill went to the desk to check out before eating.

When Bill was in line, a policeman asked, "Sir, do you know this man?"

Bill replied, "Sorry, I don't."

The policeman asked, "What about her? Seen her before?"

Bill said, "No, sir, can't say I have."

The policeman inquired, "Did you see the news this morning? These two are dead. How long have you been staying here?"

Bill looked at the policeman. "Officer, I wish I could help. I was in town for one night. I was upstairs, in bed, probably around 11:00 p.m. I went to dinner with a friend, who came back and stayed the night."

The policeman said, "Where's this friend?"

Bill replied, "See the table on the left? That's them."

The policeman asked, "Who's the woman with him?"

Bill replied, "My girlfriend—long story, but an old flame that's been rekindled. She lives in Nashville. We went for a quick dinner last evening. Afterward, she decided to spend the night. My friend was in the adjacent room."

The policeman asked, "What room were you in?"

Bill replied, "607. Why do you ask?"

The policeman became annoyed. "I'll ask the questions. This happened in Room 705, right above your room, no?"

Bill thought for a minute, having a sarcastic thought, like, *duh*, how would Room 607 be above Room 705? But self-control got the better of him.

Bill said, "I guess so. Not sure what you're driving at."

The policeman asked, "Did you hear anything last night, say between Midnight and 03:00?"

Bill replied, "Not that I recall. We had the TV on in the bedroom. It helps me fall asleep, so I doubt we would've heard anything over the TV."

The policeman looked at Bill as though he were a nuisance. "Thanks. You can go."

Bill nodded but said nothing, figuring the less said, the better. Bill got to the desk and handed in his key. The receptionist handed him a printout of the bill but didn't say anything. No big deal; it's been a hard day for them. It's not every day you've got this happening. Then Bill made his way over to the table.

Eva said, "What was that all about?"

Bill looked at Tommy wryly. "He wanted to know if I knew the deceased. Asked if we heard anything odd last night. I told him, other than Eva screaming for more, not a thing."

Eva slapped Bill's shoulder. "You didn't say that!"

Tommy said, "Can we get out of here?"

Eva said, "Tommy, can I have a moment alone with Bill first, please?"

Tommy smiled and said, "Sure."

Tommy got up from the table heading to the lobby.

Bill looked at Eva. "What's wrong?"

Eva said, "We've not talked about what's next for us."

Bill sarcastically said, "You're worried this is *wham bam, thank you, ma'am*?"

Eva smiled. "Don't be an ass. When?"

Bill replied, "When what?"

Eva sighed. "When do you want to get together again? I'm portable, so I can work remotely wherever I want. Do you want me to come back with you?"

Bill was startled at first. "You can come whenever you want, but you can drop everything that quickly? Don't you need to pack some clothes? What about Espy?"

Eva smiled. "Follow me home; I'll be packed in twenty minutes. I'll let Espy know I'm going on a trip. She's 24; she'll be fine."

Bill smiled. "I'm timing the packing. You know 20 minutes will be impossible for you."

Eva laughed. "Smart-ass. Follow me home."

As Eva and Bill walked over to Tommy, Bill said, "We're going to have an additional passenger. Apparently, she thinks I'm so irresistible she needs to come to Galveston with me."

Eva reached up, smacking Bill in the back of the head.

Eva said, "Tommy, how do you think he gets his head through doors?"

Tommy laughed. "You know, I've known him for 40+ years. You'll never meet a better marine or a better man, truly a humble guy.

I'll say this: I've never seen him this smitten before. Take care of each other."

Bill walked toward the lobby, with Eva smiling ear to ear. Bill motioned they should start moving out to the cars. They made their way through the lobby without being questioned further.

They emerged from the hotel, where Bill walked Eva to her car. "We'll follow you."

Eva said, "I'm as giddy as a schoolgirl."

Bill replied, "That's great. Let's get going."

Eva smiled as she got in her car. Bill walked over to the truck, putting his bag in the back of the bed.

When Bill got inside, Tommy asked, "What do you want to do about this?"

Bill replied, "Do about what? Is something wrong with your phone?"

Tommy looked at Bill oddly. "Are you so whipped you forgot we took Joseph's phone?"

Bill embarrassingly said, "Completely forgot. We need to remove the chip from it and then destroy the phone. We can do that at home. Also, we need to check every vehicle for a tracking device and destroy those as well."

Tommy nodded. "Eva's a pretty lady. What about Natalie?"

Bill looked at Tommy. "Never thought this would happen with Eva. Everything fell into place at dinner. It was just us, no baggage. It was the first time I felt it was packed away. As for Natalie, she's been MIA for a month. Seems like a clear sign she's not interested."

Tommy asked, "I know you've got a past with Eva. Do you think it can finally work out?"

Bill replied, "I don't know. She asked me that last night at dinner, could I finally leave the past in the past. Let's just say I'm willing to try. Who knows, maybe this time it works out. It would be a first—something working out for me in a relationship."

Eva tooted her horn while Tommy laughed. "So, it begins!"

Bill laughed as he pulled out of the parking spot, following Eva to her place. Bill was surprised it was only ten minutes away. Suddenly, it hit Bill—this was Michelle's childhood home, where Eva lived with Martinez. Bill thought, *this wouldn't be too awkward, would it?*

Tommy looked over at Bill. "Did she live here with Martinez?"

Bill replied, "Not sure. I don't remember ever being here."

Bill parked the truck as Eva made her way up to the door, putting the key into the lock.

As Tommy and Bill emerged from the truck, Bill heard Eva yell, "Seriously, you've got to be kidding me!"

Tommy looked at Bill while Bill asked, "Everything okay?"

Eva shouted, "Put some clothes on! Why are you doing that on my couch?"

Eva shut the door. "We'll need to give the lovebirds a minute to get dressed."

Tommy and Bill chuckled, clearly understanding what had happened. Eva gave them a few minutes, then reopened the door. When they went inside, Eva's daughter, Espy, was on the couch, looking flush, somewhat embarrassed, having been caught in a compromising position by her mom.

Eva said, "Espy, this is Bill and his friend Tommy."

Espy said, "The Bill!"

Eva said, "Be nice."

Espy replied, "So you're the man who helped kill my father."

Eva yelled, "Espy!"

Bill ignored her, replying, "Nice to meet you. Alcohol abuse killed your father."

Tommy mumbled under his breath, "Little bitch. Should've helped Angel meet his maker long ago—think of all the needless suffering."

Bill turned to Eva. "Okay, the clock starts now."

Eva said, "Sit in the dining room while I pack."

Espy said, "Where are you going, mama?"

Eva replied, "Galveston, two weeks. I'm staying with Bill, but please don't say anything to Michelle. We're going to tell her in our own way."

Espy said, "Whatever! The princess's wish comes true AGAIN!"

Eva went to the bedroom to pack. Tommy and Bill sat in the dining room, enjoying the quiet. Tommy pointed at a picture of the Colonel and Martinez, but Bill didn't say anything. Bill nodded to acknowledge he saw the picture.

After 15 minutes into Eva's 20 minutes, Bill got up, asking Espy, "Where's the head?"

Espy said, "Huh?"

Her Latin lover, still unintroduced, said, "Third door on the right. Across from Eva's room."

Bill saluted the lad, then headed down the hall.

When Bill got to Eva's bedroom door, he said, "Five minutes."

Eva laughed. "I'm moving as fast as I can, but I think you're right about the 20 minutes."

Bill replied, "I'm hitting the head. You do know we've got a washer and dryer in Galveston. You don't need to pack two full weeks of clothes."

Eva looked at Bill, putting her hands over her mouth. "Oh my god. You didn't just say that to me!"

Bill said, "Hang on a minute. I got to hit the head."

Bill went into the bathroom, closed the door, and did what he came to do.

When Bill emerged, he hollered, "2 minutes."

Eva sighed loudly, resuming her packing, while Bill went back to the dining room. As Bill made his way down the hallway, he heard the news report from the hotel showing a deceased woman's picture.

Suddenly, Espy shouted, "Oh my god! That's Louise."

Her boyfriend started consoling her, while Bill thought, *she's got a name.*

Eva came out of the bedroom. "What's going on?"

Espy said, "Mama, the girl on the news at the hotel, it's Louise, the girl I babysat for."

Eva sighed, looking at Espy. "I'm sorry, honey, but you haven't babysat for her in a while."

Espy replied, "I know, but still. It's hard to believe she's wrapped up in this."

Eva said, "I know, honey. It's always hard to lose someone that young, but you said she was into drugs the last time you saw her, right?"

Espy didn't respond, while Eva went over to comfort her. Bill was sensitive to the situation but also realized they had a long drive ahead of them.

After 10 minutes, Eva said, "Listen, I'll be gone for two weeks. There's plenty in the fridge. If you need me, call me on my cell. Love you."

Espy suddenly unphased, "Okay, have a nice trip."

Eva motioned to Bill. It was time to go. Bill grabbed her bag, making their way through the front door, where Bill placed Eva's bag in the flatbed along with his own.

Bill looked over at Tommy. "Tracking devices!"

Eva said, "What?"

Bill walked toward Eva's vehicle, got on the ground, and found the tracking device inside the wheel well by the right rear tire. He got up, heading back to his truck. Bill showed the device to Tommy.

Eva said, "What's that?"

Bill replied, "Tracking device. It's part of the story, so I'll leave it till then. All set?"

Tommy said, "No. Where's the dip?"

Bill replied, "Oh yeah. We'll need it for the long drive."

Both hopped out for a second, loading up with dip for the long ride home.

After they jumped back in the truck, Eva said, "Disgusting!"

Unphased by Eva's comment, Tommy grabbed an empty Coke bottle and spat into it. Bill did the same as Bill put the truck in drive, heading back to the highway. They had a long road ahead.

Suffice it to say, it was going to be a long day.

Chapter 28
Early December 2024

On the ride back, they stopped in Tuscaloosa, AL to get something to eat, stopping at a local fast-food joint that served burgers, chicken fried steaks, and even some barbecue. After they finished eating, Eva headed to the lady's room, thinking they were about to get back on the road.

Bill asked Tommy, "Can you grab the check? I'm going to call Jenn."

Tommy nodded. "Be careful. You don't know how she's involved in this."

Bill hadn't told Tommy about the one-night stand with Jenn a week ago. At this moment, it wasn't important, but his concern wasn't lost on Bill. He felt she was involved in this, too, but how?

Bill said, "Got it, be back in a minute."

Bill headed out the front door, not before running into Eva returning to the table.

Eva asked, "Where are you going?"

Bill replied, "Calling Jenn. Look, there's something I haven't told you. I know the timing's strange."

Eva got a serious look on her face. "You didn't sleep with her again."

Bill looked at Eva, thinking it was figures she guessed.

Bill said, "Yes. It was before I came to Nashville. She showed up at the house, frightened and alone. I thought I was doing something nice by letting her stay one night. That night, I had one of my bad dreams. Jenn came upstairs to check on me, then it just happened. I'm not telling you this to hurt you. I'm trying to be honest with you."

Eva was getting angry, but she tempered her reply. "It hurts to know you were with her. But it happened before you came up to Nashville. It will never happen again, right?"

Bill replied, "Correct. I came out here to confront her on these new facts. I'm concerned she's using this boy to get to Michelle or something worse."

Eva looked a little stunned. "Don't you think that's a reach?"

Bill responded, "I'll know when I see her. You've got no idea what she's capable of, but I do. If she feels the pressure, she'll make a mistake. She always does."

Eva nodded, kissing Bill on the cheek, heading inside to be with Tommy. Bill figured she'd listen to the call, but this was probably better. Bill pulled out his phone and called Jenn.

Jenn picked up on the first ring. "Hey, I was thinking about you today."

Bill replied, "Really? Look I've got a question. I want a straight answer!"

Jenn said, "Okay, sounds ominous."

Bill responded, "My daughter met a boy at UT and had their first date the other night. Things went well. The boy was nice, polite."

Jenn replied, "That's sweet. You called to tell me about your daughter's love life?"

Bill replied, "When I asked for the boy's name and where he came from, my daughter told me his name was Patrick McTiernay, raised in Montana. That can't be a coincidence, not in a million years."

Jenn was quiet for a minute. "He's my son. I named him after his father."

Bill said, "You told me you never remarried or had children again! His father's name is Patrick?"

Jenn replied, "I named him after you. His full name is William Patrick McTiernay. He goes by Patrick."

Bill replied, "Are you telling me Patrick's my son? Impossible, we hadn't had sex for over a year before BJ's death!"

Jenn said, "You don't remember this, but a few days before BJ passed away, you came home from a work event very drunk. Do you remember that?"

Bill replied, "No. I don't."

Jenn continued, "When you got home, you were in a very playful mood. We connected like we did in the past when things were terrific. We made love that night; Patrick was the result. I had him in witness protection."

Bill was getting angry. "You told me Owen was the father, when you were begging to stay on my benefits, if I recall? I've seen you twice in the last two years, asking if you ever remarried or had children. You told me you didn't."

Jenn said, "Bill, I'm sorry. I didn't know how to tell you. We told Patrick his father was dead. I told him his father died before he was born but didn't offer specifics."

Bill replied, "So let me get this straight. I knocked you up in a drunken haze that I don't remember. Eighteen years later, a kid shows up in my daughter's life, neither of which knows they're brother and sister, and you're sorry?"

Jenn coldly replied, "Didn't know how to tell you. Over the years, I thought of telling you, but too many things would've been compromised. I was protecting my son. You, of all people, understand that, no?"

Bill thought for a moment. "Perhaps, but how do I know he's my son?"

Jenn responded, "It could only have been you; Owen couldn't father a child, the result of an accident when he was young. The doctors told him at 14 that he'd never have kids of his own."

Bill shouted, "I can't believe it. Why did you tell me then that Owen was the father."

Jenn said, "I thought things were over with us, so I said it to hurt you. What do you want to do now?"

Bill replied, "I don't believe you. We need to tell the kids. It's not fair to them. I'd rather be wrong waiting on a DNA test than for two of them to get together. No good comes of that."

Jenn said, "Agreed. I'm in Austin for a few days. Come up, and we'll sort it out."

Bill said, "Jenn, if you're lying to me, I swear, I'll kill you myself!"

Jenn cut Bill off, shooting back, "No need to get nasty."

Bill replied, "I'm heading to Austin. I'm not alone; Tommy and Eva are with me."

Jenn said, "I was sorry to hear about Joseph."

Bill thought for a moment, wondering how Jenn knew about a man killed in Nashville who had no identification, while she was in Austin. Bill decided to play it cool.

Bill said, "Not sure what you're talking about."

Jenn said, "Didn't you hear on the news he was killed in Nashville? Apparently, killed by a prostitute in a bad drug deal. It was all over the news this morning."

Bill replied, "Didn't know that. Sounds awful, but nobody from the family has called. Look, I've got to run. I'll call you when I'm close to Austin."

Jenn replied, "Okay, see you soon."

Bill answered, "Yes. Remember, Eva and Tommy are with me."

Jenn said, "So it's Eva that's won the Bill Sweepstakes? Lucky girl."

Bill replied, "Whatever, see you in Austin. We'll talk about a DNA test when I arrive."

Then Bill hung up, heading back inside.

When Bill got back to the table, he said, "Ready? Tommy, hope you don't mind, but we're stopping in Austin before heading home."

Tommy said, "Skipper, are you okay? I've seen that look. Only Jenn can piss you off like that."

Before Bill could answer, Eva asked, "Did it go ok?"

Tommy sarcastically said, "Well, if any woman could make him look like that, it's Jenn."

Bill calmly said, "Let's get going. We can talk about it in the truck. Eva, I'm going to preface this with, there's been an interesting development."

Eva replied, "What development?"

Bill replied, "Let's do this in the truck."

At this point, Tommy starts to get up from the table, and Eva followed suit. Then, they made their way to the truck.

As Bill started the truck, he said, "Jenn told me she's got a son. His name is William Patrick McTiernay, and he goes by Patrick, he goes to school at UT in Austin. She just informed me that he's my son. Lastly, she passed along her condolences for Joseph's loss, but I've got no idea how she knew. She played it off like it was all over the news, but I scrolled the news feeds; they haven't identified him yet."

Tommy sat in the front seat, stunned, while loading up with some dip.

Tommy handed Bill the tin. "Think you're going to need this."

Bill nodded, but his attention was on Eva in the backseat. She didn't say anything for almost two minutes. She sat with her hands over her mouth in shock.

Bill asked, "Eva, are you okay?"

Eva finally said, "I don't know what to say. You said you weren't intimate for a year before it ended?"

Bill replied, "From what Jenn said, a few days before BJ's death, I apparently came home drunk from a work event, and she said we had sex that night. I don't remember that. I told her we've got to do a DNA test to be sure. Who knows if it's true? That's why we're heading to Austin."

Tommy asked, "Thought Owen was the father?"

Bill said, "According to Jenn, Owen shot blanks. Said she told me Owen was the father to hurt me. She said I was the only man she was with before BJ's death. Honestly, I don't know what to believe. We need to put a stop to Michelle's relationship. It's unfair if it's true."

Eva blurted out, "Can we just drive, please!"

Bill replied, "Sure. I wanted you to know. I promised to tell you the truth."

Eva said, "I know, but you're testing my resolve today."

Bill shot back, "I found out about this five minutes ago. Let's not try to connect all the wires and go crazy before we've got a reason."

Eva shot Bill a nasty look from the backseat, which Bill clearly saw in the rearview mirror. Bill put the truck in drive. Off to Austin they went.

Chapter 29
Early December 2024

The ride to Austin was quiet. Tommy fell asleep 30 minutes after leaving Tuscaloosa while Eva continued staring out the window. They rode quietly for the first hour before Bill put on the radio to have some background noise to keep going, with the dip helping in that regard.

Bill intentionally didn't say anything, as he knew Eva was processing this latest body shot. Hell, it was a body shot to Bill, but if they were going to rekindle this relationship, he didn't want any secrets—or at least not anymore. He hadn't yet explained everything.

Also, Bill started to consider Eva's motives for the reunion. Why, after all this time? Was she lonely? Did she still love him? While he's been willing to entertain a reunion, he also thought he needed to be cautious, develop trust.

Tommy slept most of the ride to Austin, waking up 30 minutes before arriving. Eva fell asleep in the backseat along the way, too, but at least she wasn't snoring like Tommy.

After Tommy woke up, he asked, "Okay, Skipper?"

Bill replied, "Fine. What else can happen with Jenn after all this time?"

Tommy asked, "Do you think this is a setup, another way to draw you out?"

Bill said, "I've got to tell you, I've been considering the possibility. She's capable of anything. She knew my Uncle Jack back when we were in basic. Anything's possible with her."

Tommy said, "I know she can't be trusted. What do you want to do, Skipper?"

Bill knew what he wanted to say: Drive Jenn out to the middle of nowhere, leave her for dead near a pack of wild dogs, but self-control got the better of him.

However, Bill said, "Don't know yet. We need to assess the situation first."

Tommy said, "I never told you this, but Amanda never cared for Jenn. We knew you loved her, but we never thought she was right for you. Also, what was the conversation you had with Eva before making the call to Jenn? Looked intense."

Bill replied, "I told her Jenn came for a visit a few days ago before we came up to Nashville. Jenn gave me some bullshit about being slapped around by who she suspected was Joseph at the airport not long after the thing with Natalie occurred. She came to the house late, seemingly petrified. Anyway, I let her sleep downstairs. That night, I had a night terror; you know the day. Jenn came up to check on me, and it just happened."

Tommy laughed. "You banged Jenn for old-time's sake. How did you let that happen? Also, I'm not seeing her angle."

Bill thought for a minute. "Do you think the witness protection was a lie? Perhaps she sent Seamus to Austin on a mission, then Patrick once Seamus was compromised. Perhaps this Patrick's another plant to draw me out, slogging me through the mud for Jenn's amusement."

Tommy said, "Why after all this time? I would've thought the Owen thing would've been enough reason to draw you out."

Bill replied, "Perhaps. Also, I don't know how she knew about Michelle before I told her. I wonder if she's had any contact with Joseph. Maybe he's the link? She knew him before we met. I recalled her telling me the second time she surprised me in Galveston. Hell, my place has been like the fucking Grand Central Station of the crazy these past two years."

Tommy asked, "You think she's been in contact with Joseph all this time?"

Bill responded, "Interesting question. I don't know, but it's something we need to figure out. Wait, we've got his phone; let's have a look at that. Let me call Michelle to let her know we're going to be in town."

Tommy nodded while Bill rang Michelle. Tommy grabbed Joseph's phone to start looking closer at it.

Michelle picked up on the third ring. "Hey, Dad, what's up?"

Bill replied, "Got a surprise. We'll be in Austin in 20 minutes. Had some business to tend to, thought we might surprise you."

Michelle said, "We? Whose we?"

Bill said, "Tommy and Mom."

Michelle said, "Mom's with you guys? What's going on? Espy called and left me a message saying I'd be happy about something soon. But it made no sense."

Bill replied, "Tommy and I were in Nashville for the night. Mom and I went for dinner. That's all that happened."

Michelle said, "I knew that. She told me. Okay, but it's a good start, no?"

Bill said, "When you told your mom about Patrick, we decided to come meet the lad. Rip the band-aid off, so to speak."

Michelle paused nervously. "Uhm, okay. We're in the library now. His mom is in town, too. He was going to introduce me to her; perhaps we could make a gathering of it."

Bill replied, "Sure. But we've got some things to iron out tonight. Be prepared."

Michelle shot back, "That sounds strange. What do you mean?"

Bill said, "We'll discuss it when we're there. I'll text you when we're in the hotel room."

Michelle said, "Okay. Love you, see you soon."

Bill responded, "Love you too."

Then Bill hung up. Eva woke up while Bill was on the phone with Michelle, hearing the entire conversation.

Eva asked, "How are you going to break this to her?"

Bill said, "Gently. I'm hoping she's not too serious with this boy."

Eva asked, "Do you want me to tell her?"

Bill replied, "Let's do it together."

Eva said, "She's going to be crushed."

Bill said, "She'll get over it. How long's the relationship— a month, maybe?"

Eva replied, "Think about it: You find out the boy you're gaga over is your long-lost brother. That's a little crushing, no?"

Bill responded, "Perhaps. Potentially disgusting if things have progressed physically."

Eva shouted, "That's gross. She told me they haven't been together like that. Thank God."

Bill found it interesting that Eva never brought up the fact that they were having dinner with Jenn, ending the conversation after the gross comment about Patrick.

They headed over the 6th Street Bridge toward the hotel. Bill stopped near the front entrance, opening his door, then Eva's door, unloading the luggage before getting the ticket from the valet. Bill tipped the valet $10, then headed inside, making their way to the front desk.

Bill told the concierge, "Checking in. Quinn. Two rooms, one with an adjacent door."

The concierge took Bill's credit card, along with his driver's license, then handed him the keys to both rooms.

The concierge said, "Mr. Quinn, thanks for being a repeat visitor. Is there anything else I can assist you with?"

Bill replied, "I hope so. We need to make reservations for tonight, say 19:00. We're going to be a party of 6. Is that something you can help me with?"

The concierge said, "Of course. Let me look... yep, got a table for six at 7 p.m. Anything else I can assist with?"

Bill said, "No. Thanks."

The concierge replied, "You're welcome; enjoy your stay with us."

Bill didn't say anything as they moved away from the front desk, heading to the elevators and then up to the rooms.

Eva asked, "What's the room number?"

Bill replied, "We're in 2307, Tommy's in 2308. Room with an adjacent door."

When they got to the room, it was 17:30. Bill thought perhaps they'd get a nap before heading down for dinner. Once they were situated, Eva and Bill were alone in their room.

Eva asked, "I heard you talking about Jenn in the car when I was waking up, so I heard a little of what you were discussing. What's going on?"

Bill said, "Honestly, I'm not sure. I'm missing something. Part of me feels it's a setup, but a setup for what or from whom? I'm still trying to put the pieces together. Does any of this make sense?"

Eva replied, "Not sure. I don't know her the way you do. How do you feel about having another son?"

Bill responded, "I don't know. Perhaps if it's true, I'll feel the same way about him I did about Michelle. Right now, we need to make them aware of the possibility, then get a DNA test done. If Jenn's using this as a setup—meaning he isn't my son, using him as a decoy to draw me out—that's an act of war. She'll meet the same fate as Owen and Seamus."

Eva sat up on the bed, looking at Bill. "You think she's somehow trying to get at you after all this time? For what reason? And don't give me this BS about it being all in the story you've yet to tell. You said if we're in a relationship, we need to trust each other and tell each other things—warts and all. The time's come. I need to know, as I need to protect Michelle, especially if something happened to you."

Bill laid back on the bed, taking a deep sigh.

Bill sat up while Eva said, "We're in this together. Me, you, Michelle, hell, even Patrick, if it comes to it. We'll be one proud but fucked-up family."

Eva stared at him, having the look of I'm waiting.

Bill shook his head. "Okay, you want the story! I'm going to tell you, repeat it once for Michelle. Afterwards, it will be put away—FOREVER."

Eva said, "Finally, lay it on me!"

Bill began the story by telling Eva he had left several things out when describing his service, Tommy, Fred, and Mike, all in the same squad, his interactions with the Colonel and Martinez, as well as the weapons cache seizures of the Mexican truck loaders. He told her he'd seen Eva's picture on the back of the Colonel's CP many years before they met in Nashville. He told her about being with Fatima that night.

At first, she took it all in. By Bill's count, he was 25 double hands over the mouth at this point, while he wasn't even close to done. He continued, going into meeting protecting Jenn at Uncle Jack's pub, meeting Jenn on campus, Boston, Boston's aftermath, and what happened when they were married, cutting himself off from his family.

Eva said, "So you killed three men in Boston to protect Jenn, a woman you loved."

Bill replied, "Yes. Given the situation, us or them. Given that choice, easy—always them."

Eva nodded. "So, how'd things wrap up after Boston? If you thought she was nuts, why did you stay with her?"

Bill said, "All I'll say is, things were great after Boston, just about to start at the Firm. She was wrapped up in her nursing studies, and we developed a decent marriage for ten years, but that all changed after BJ was born, it started during the pregnancy in my opinion. It was like a switch went off inside her head, going from a responsible adult to a pesky teenager. It was like she regressed."

Then, he went into details on Owen, the kidnapping, finding BJ. Eva tried to be stoic, listening intently, trying not to break Bill's rhythm in telling the story.

Bill told her about the morning of BJ's death, calling Eva that morning as well as the guilt he felt in the moment, how Jenn let Owen in the house, the video footage of Owen knocking Jenn out, watching Owen stand over his son, then kidnapping him. He talked about the phone call Owen made to him before finding BJ's body, then he went into the funeral plans. He finished with the events at the funeral before Eva arrived that day.

Bill stopped, saying, "As screwed up as this sounds, the best part of the whole situation was when you came up for BJ's funeral. You know I had to pull away from you when you hugged me. I got a little excited."

Eva said, "You remember that? I wasn't sure you noticed it. I did."

Bill shrugged his shoulders, then went into getting his revenge on Owen, telling her he had some help but wouldn't reveal who. She guessed it was Tommy, but Bill never confirmed. Bill told Eva about Uncle Jack's proposition.

Eva broke in. "So, Uncle Jack helped you take your revenge."

Bill replied, "Yes, for a price. The proposition wouldn't be paid unless Owen was delivered alive. However, when we did the drop-off, you know who was there to greet us?"

Eva replied, "Why don't I want to know?"

Bill said, "The delivery was to Martinez and the Colonel. Owen screwed with one of the weapons caches in connection to the Mexican cartels. Uncle Jack gave me my revenge by being the delivery man. I wanted to kill the bastard so badly, but I didn't. I put one hell of a beating on Owen, but we delivered him alive. Uncle Jack's promise was so good that I couldn't pass it up. Besides, the Mexican cartels were far more ruthless to their victims."

Eva stopped in her tracks. "You're telling me Angel and the Colonel got rid of Owen."

Bill said, "Yes. It was their order, which I filled so many years prior. Owen stole from them. I was told Owen ended up in a 50-gallon oil drum."

Eva asked, "This wasn't long after BJ died, right?"

Bill replied, "Next day. Came home from the funeral, planned it out. Delivered him the following morning. Two hours from start to finish."

Eva looked numb. "I remember not long after BJ died, Angel and the Colonel were on our back patio talking about how well the Skipper did getting rid of the rat. You're the Skipper."

Bill said, "Yes. Let me continue. We're only halfway there."

Eva nodded as Bill reminisced with her about the wonderful times they had in Nashville. Bill told Eva how much it hurt when it ended, informing her of the Colonel's visit the night it ended. Bill talked about leaving for the last time, always wondering if Michelle was his daughter.

Bill tried to describe how he felt inside, the pure joy to know that Michelle was his daughter. The whole time, Eva sat quiet, listening to the rest of the story as tears streamed down her face. She sensed Bill needed the space to tell it without 500 questions. Bill went into Seamus on the trip back from Austin, then the shootout at home. Bill told her how Joseph kept interceding in the Seamus thing.

Bill finally said, "I didn't have a choice. They came at what I loved. I protected my family with whatever means I had at my disposal. In a sense, I was back in combat, living and fighting for my squad, nothing mattered more."

Eva said, "I get it. We're your squad now. I love you for that. You know, you can't make this shit up."

Bill replied, "No, you can't."

Eva asked, "What happened with Joseph?"

Bill said, "I think he was selling himself to the feds. He said a man named Tavares was talking about what happened to Owen and Seamus. I believe he made up the Tavares betrayal to cover his own betrayal. Again, he threatened my family, so I dealt with it."

Eva nodded, then asked, "What about Jenn?"

Bill said, "Got to figure out if it's a setup or if she's telling the truth about Patrick. She's a consummate liar, so anything's possible."

Eva looked at Bill, kissing him softly. "We'll figure this out. I love you. It's 6:45, and we need to head down for dinner."

Bill nodded, getting up. "The boxes are closed until I tell Michelle. How do you think she'll react?"

Eva smiled. "Thanks for finally telling me. You're right, it was ugly. Hopefully, this thing with Jenn is a bad series of coincidences. As for Michelle, she'll love you even more. Loyalty to those she loves is something she learned from you despite you not being in her life for so long. She always had your personality. Since she met you, that's always one of the things she's admired about you most. Family first, always!"

Bill shrugged his shoulders as if to say, *who knows*? Before they headed downstairs, Bill grabbed a blazer, placing his XDA 45ACP into the back of his belt. Eva had gone to the bathroom, so she didn't see him gather his weapon. For some reason, Bill was on high alert, feeling the need to be prepared—his sixth sense. Unfortunately, when his sixth sense is right, it never ends well.

After Eva finished in the bathroom, they headed downstairs for dinner. When getting on the elevator, Bill thought it was odd: after telling Eva the story, he didn't feel relieved or satisfied. In fact, Bill felt more guarded, anxious that the next shoe was about to drop.

Perhaps Tommy was right—Bill should've buried these boxes a long time ago without sharing them with anyone.

Chapter 31
Early December 2024

When Bill and Eva reached the lobby, they headed over to the restaurant. Tommy, Michelle, Patrick, and Jenn were already seated at the table, not having much of a conversation, it appeared. Tommy had a look on his face like he wanted to strangle Jenn. When Eva and Bill reached the table, Michelle stood up along with Patrick, greeting them.

Patrick said, "Mr. Quinn, nice to meet you. Michelle talks about you both all the time."

Bill thought to himself, *kiss-ass.*

Bill heard Tommy mumble under his breath, "Pussy."

Bill tried to contain his laughter as Patrick asked, "Is everything okay, sir?"

Bill replied, "I'm fine. Don't call me sir, Bill. Calling me sir is like putting an elevator in an outhouse."

Patrick gave a complimentary laugh, kiss-ass that he was, then turned toward Jenn.

Michelle said, "Dad, Mom, this is Patrick's mom, Jenn."

Jenn glared at Bill to see what he might say next, but he said plainly, "It's nice to see you."

Bill thought for a moment, *she's playing it cool*. The waiter came over to take their drink orders, then regaled them with specials on the menu.

The waiter said, "I'll get you the drinks while you look over the menu."

As the waiter went over to the bar, Patrick asked, "How was your recent trip?"

Bill thought for a second—how did he know? Bill quickly tried to remember if he told Michelle where their destination was, but he couldn't recall.

Bill finally said, "It was fine. How'd you know about our trip?"

Patrick replied, "Michelle told me you were in Nashville."

Michelle replied strangely, "I don't remember telling you that."

Patrick hedged, "Maybe I overheard your conversation with your dad."

Bill nodded, unimpressed with his prissiness.

Bill could tell Michelle was extremely nervous, while Eva was cold, saying nothing and just sharing glaring looks with Jenn. Jenn only engaged with Bill or the kids. Bill found the ladies' stare-down amusing, but it made the dinner as uncomfortable as possible. It was the quietest catfight he'd ever seen. Tommy, on the other hand, kept looking at Jenn, softly shaking his head, clearly plotting several ways of getting rid of her. Michelle looked at Eva, thinking, *What's wrong?* The tension was so thick you could cut it with a knife.

Michelle asked, "Dad, when are you taking Mom back to Nashville?"

Bill looked at Eva, and then Eva replied, "I'm spending two weeks in Galveston. I'm sorry this is the way you're finding out, but today's been full of surprises."

Michelle smiled. "Really. I thought I'd never see the day. Surprises? What do you mean?"

Eva looked at Bill. "I'm tired of this bullshit, Bill, let's get this over with."

Jenn then blurted out, "This isn't the first time we've all met..."

Bill cut her off. "Michelle, Jenn's my ex-wife, BJ's mother."

Michelle pulled her vintage Eva, hands over her mouth, looking at Patrick. "Your mom was married to my dad about 35 years ago? Did you know that?"

Bill thought Patrick seemed only a little surprised by this development, sensing his reaction wasn't completely genuine.

Patrick looked at Jenn nervously. "Mom, you told me my father was dead."

Jenn calmly replied, "We wanted to tell you together."

Patrick said, "Hang on a second. I'm 19, Michelle's 18, only a few months apart. You said you had been pregnant before your first husband left. Is this my dad?"

The table fell silent, but Bill remained calm, forcing Jenn to answer the question. Bill wasn't letting her off the hook, as only she knew the truth. Also, Jenn told Bill she had told her son that his father had died, not left. The stories didn't add up.

Eva whispered to Bill, "This isn't awkward at all."

Bill whispered back, "I know."

But Jenn still had not responded.

Patrick in a phony, prissy manner, exclaimed, "Mom, answer me!"

Jenn finally said, "Yes, Bill's your father."

Bill then chimed in, "I'm sorry if this comes across coldly, but we need a DNA test to confirm. I'm not sure I believe it."

Bill left it there. This situation was already on fire, and bringing Owen into the mix would've been the incendiary to light the place ablaze. Until...

Tommy asked, "Why couldn't Owen be the father?"

The table fell silent, motionless. Again, Jenn had the ball.

Jenn looked over at Tommy. "You know, I never liked you or your wife."

Tommy sarcastically said, "Oh, that hurts. We've spent countless hours up all night worrying about what you thought of us, you bitch."

"You were nothing but trouble then, nothing but trouble now. Skipper was fucking blind to you. Amanda said it all the time."

Michelle cut in, trying to be the adult. "Let's calm down. This is getting us nowhere…"

Jenn looked at Michelle. "Listen, little missy, shut the …"

Bill cut Jenn off. "Don't you ever talk to my daughter like that? Who do you think you are? You set this whole thing up, didn't you?"

Jenn initially said nothing, then Eva wanted to be the next county heard from. "I'm sorry, but I don't see any similarities between Bill or Jenn, none whatsoever."

Tommy then said, "You know what, you're right!"

Jenn was now panicking and decided it was time to retreat, getting up from the table.

Jenn said, "Goodnight, let's never do this again."

Bill combatively said, "Wait, you wanted this, now you're running away? Coward, you always were. When the going got tough, you bailed, then ran to Owen for aid. Same old Jenn, just no Owen to run home to! Maybe your son here can provide that comfort."

Jenn had a fire in her eyes, attempting to drive them through Bill.

Jenn shouted back, "You know I could always take you out. You know why!"

Bill stood up from the table. "Any time you want a shot at the title, just name the place and I'll be here!"

Jenn looked at Eva. "Good luck with that old marine warhorse!"

Eva said, "Thanks. I'm sure we'll be happier together than you two ever were. We could fall off a log and improve upon that."

Jenn shouted at Eva, "Slut, you're a fucking homewrecker. You broke up our marriage."

Eva sat in amazement, composing herself, then finally said, "You're the one that screwed up your marriage. We found each other out of sheer circumstance because of the shitty relationships we had at home. You killed your marriage, even your first son, by letting Owen in the house that morning. Don't lay your shit at my feet. You've got some nerve!"

Tommy shouted, "Eva, good for you; I wasn't sure you had the stones! Bill, I got a lot of respect for her. Good for you!"

At this point, Jenn moved away from the table, heading out of the restaurant. Patrick sat in shock, not knowing what to say, while Michelle was in tears.

Michelle mumbled a few times, "I almost slept with my brother."

After a few minutes of silence, the waiter came over. "We've been holding your meals. Is it okay to bring it over?"

Bill surprisingly said, "Yes. I'm not sure about anyone else, but I'm hungry."

Michelle looked up, shocked. "Dad, how can you eat after that?"

Bill replied, "Sunshine, I haven't eaten all day. If you want, go upstairs with Mom to settle down. Patrick, you're welcome to stay, but I'm assuming you've got more questions for Jenn."

Patrick said, "I'm going to head back. Do you want any money for dinner?"

Bill replied, "No. Tell your *MOM*, I want this DNA test done immediately."

Patrick nodded, excusing himself from the table attempting to hug Michelle as he left, but Michelle pushed him away.

Eva said, "Michelle, let's go upstairs. Bill, box up our dinners, please. We might get hungry later."

Bill winked, replying, "Sure thing, sunshine."

Eva smiled at being called sunshine, sensing Bill was satisfied with how she handled all this. Then Eva and Michelle made their way to the elevators. Tommy and Bill remained at the table eating dinner, not letting a good meal go to waste because of Jenn.

As they dug in, Tommy asked, "Now what? I'll tell you this: I'd cut off my left testicle if that kid's yours. No way in the world."

A little surprised by Tommy's comment, Bill replied, "Not sure what to say to that. As it relates to Jenn, we need to find out more. Something isn't adding up."

Tommy asked, "What are you thinking?"

Bill replied, "He could be my son, maybe some characteristics from Jenn's side of the family, only met her father once. Second, maybe he's not my son. Maybe she's paying him to get close to Michelle, either to hurt her or get to me. That's as far as my thinking's taken me."

Tommy replied, "You know, back when Owen disappeared, I told Amanda my only regret was not getting rid of her at the same time. Knowing she was part of the kidnapping."

Bill shot him a look. "Perhaps. Think of all the needless suffering that would've ended."

Tommy and Bill finished their dinner, paid the bill, and carried the food back for the girls.

When they arrived at the room, Bill asked Tommy, "Still got Joseph's phone?"

Tommy replied, "Yeah, why?"

Bill replied, "Want to check something."

Tommy asked, "What are you thinking?"

Bill said, "A third possibility. I don't want to say it, but Joseph's phone could provide the clue."

Bill entered the room, finding Eva holding Michelle, as Michelle sobbed in her arms. She must've really fallen for this prissy little shit. Eventually, she'd figure it out, as we've all picked winners when we were dating.

Bill reached down, putting his hand on Michelle's head. "I know it's tough, but you're going to be okay. I promise."

Michelle continued to cry but said nothing, nodding, acknowledging he was trying to comfort her. Tommy came through the adjacent door, handing Bill Joseph's phone. Eva was too busy with Michelle, so she didn't notice Tommy had passed the phone to Bill.

Bill told Eva, "I'm sorry to leave you right now, but I need some air."

Eva said, "Okay, she needs me more right now."

Bill said, "I know. I'll be back in a little while."

Chapter 32
Early December 2024

Bill headed out the front door toward his truck, looking for his tin of dip. When he got to the truck and found the tin, he loaded up the left side of his mouth. Bill had the Coke bottle in the cup holder of the truck to use as well.

It was a rainy, cold night, so Bill started the truck and looked through Joseph's phone. When Bill turned on the phone, there were 100 missed calls, with nearly as many texts. When he looked at the log, most of the missed calls were from Joseph's wife. Bill noticed one of the calls was received less than an hour ago.

Bill continued to comb through the call log, noticing a 406-area code number. Bill compared the number to his phone, confirming it was Jenn's cell. Bill scrolled through the rest of the log, noticing a 615-area code. His heart dropped momentarily, thinking Eva had been in contact with Joseph. However, when Bill compared Eva's number, they were different. Bill decided to ring the 615 number. After three rings, a young woman answered.

The woman said, "Hey, Joey Bear, Espy's here. Wondered when I'd hear from you."

Bill hung up the phone. Eva's daughter was in contact with Joseph. Bill couldn't believe it, now thinking back to the act she put on with the dead girl in Nashville. Bill went through Joseph's photo log on the phone, noticing pictures of a lot of young girls dressed provocatively. He saw five photos of Espy, where she wore less in the picture than her mom ever wore to bed for Bill. It was a troubling sight.

Bill texted Tommy, "Can you join me downstairs?"

Tommy replied, "Sure, where?"

Bill replied, "Truck, I need to show you something."

Tommy texted, "Be right down."

As Bill waited for Tommy, Joseph's phone rang again. It was his wife, leaving the 100th voicemail of the day. While waiting for Tommy, Bill looked at the tracking app on the phone, reviewing each number and assessing identities where he could. Other than Jenn and Espy, Bill didn't have any other similar contacts. A couple of the numbers were from the tracking devices they'd already dismantled, one from Eva's car and one from Bill's truck. Tommy came to the passenger side window while Bill unlocked the door, and Tommy climbed in.

Tommy said, "What's going on?"

Bill said, "Been looking at his call log, found Jenn's number, numerous calls. Found Eva's daughter's number, too. Jenn's been in contact for several months, looking at the phone log, while Espy rang him today. I noticed this 615-area code, but it wasn't Eva's number. I called the number, and Espy picked up the phone, sounding drunk and forward—kind of like they were involved in some way. Also, look at the photos—there are a lot of young girls. Can you see them here? There are five of Espy alone. Eva never wore that to bed for me."

Tommy said, "This gets better by the minute. How's Eva going to take it?"

Bill replied, "Honestly, I don't know. Don't know the involvement between Joseph and Espy. That's got me nervous. I don't understand the connection."

Tommy then asked the fateful question, "Can we finally eliminate this bitch? Please don't give me any crap about wanting to confront her. Let's put us all out of our misery!"

Bill was a little surprised, realizing Tommy was pissed, understanding, but what if Patrick was his son? If Bill was going to do that to Jenn, he'd have a hard time doing it to him, too. Suddenly, Joseph's phone rang, a 406 number, but it wasn't one that had been logged before.

Bill answered the phone, like Uncle Jack would have. "Speak!"

The voice on the phone said, "Joseph, it's Patrick, glad we caught you. Been reaching out all day. Bill figured Jenn was lying about everything. He's pretty sure I'm a plant, too. The fucker demanded a DNA test. What do you want me to do?"

Bill paused for a moment, then emulating Joseph's Brooklyn accent, "This was Jenn's deal; you went along with it. Talk to Jenn about it. You're both in Austin. Take care of it!"

Bill heard Patrick whispering to Jenn.

Bill heard Jenn say, "Hang up the phone!"

Patrick didn't hang up the phone. Instead, he panicked.

Patrick said to Jenn, "This was your idea, using Michelle to get to Bill. You wanted revenge. I went along because I'd get the girl plus the inheritance. There's no payday anymore."

Tommy and Bill sat in the truck, listening to the proverbial rattlesnakes committing suicide. As they continued, Bill plotted the next steps in his mind.

Patrick then yelled, "What do you want to do now?"

Jenn said, "Hang up the phone. You don't know if it's Joseph! He's never been off the grid like this!"

Bill winked at Tommy. "Go smooth it over. Make him feel he can be secure in your friendship. Then, continue as planned. I want my money back from that prick."

Patrick said, "How?"

Bill angrily replied, "Figure it out. You've been paid for this. You cozied up to the girl; do the same with him."

Patrick replied, "Okay, I'll talk it over with Jenn."

At this point, Bill hung up the phone.

Tommy looked at Bill. "What else do you need?"

Bill replied, "When they call back, we'll set up a meeting, leave the girls behind, then take care of this. I'm done."

Tommy said, "Finally."

Bill said, "We need to tell Eva. She's got to protect Michelle and Espy."

Tommy said, "Agreed. She'll have no problem participating after this evening's calamity."

With that, they headed back to the room. When they went upstairs, Eva and Michelle were asleep on the bed. Bill decided not to wake them, as they looked peaceful after such a difficult day. Telling them about this wasn't going to be easy.

Bill grabbed a pillow, headed to the couch, placing the pillow on it, and then laid down, trying to close his eyes to rest. As he began to fall asleep, Eva came out into the living room. Bill heard the bedroom door close behind her.

Eva said, "Honey, why are you out here?"

Bill replied, "Both of you were sound asleep, so I figured I'd let you sleep. You're going to need your rest for tomorrow."

Eva asked, "What happened after you left?"

Bill responded, "Recon. There are a few things I need to tell you."

Eva sarcastically said, "Go on!"

Bill continued, "We took Joseph's mobile phone last night. That's how we knew about the tracking devices. I'm sorry but I forgot that when I told you the story. Tonight, I went through the call logs and noticed two suspicious numbers. One's a 406-area code, the other a 615-area code. 406 is the area code for Montana, cross-referenced the number, and it was Jenn's cell. The 615-area code number I couldn't cross-reference, so I called it. A girl picked up saying, 'Hello, Joey Bear, Espy here.'"

Eva was flabbergasted. "You're kidding me, Espy's involved in this?"

Bill said, "Dead serious. What's Espy's number?"

Eva hurriedly grabbed her phone, pulling up Espy's contact information.

Bill said, "Sorry, but it's a match."

Eva sank into Bill on the couch, crying.

Eva asked, "What does this mean?"

Bill said, "I don't know. Perhaps she wasn't involved. Maybe she's the connection to the girl that overdosed. Maybe she's involved somehow. The tone of her response seemed more like a romantic interest than a business one. There were five provocative photos of her on Joseph's phone. Let's just say you never wore that to bed for me on our Nashville nights."

Bill showed Eva the pictures of Espy.

Eva said, "I can't believe this. I need to call her now."

Bill replied, "Hang on, if she's involved, she could be in danger. They're scrambling, not knowing what happened to Joseph. When I was in the truck with Tommy, we got a call from another 406-area code. I answered, pretending to be Joseph. Bottom line, this whole thing's a setup. Get close to Michelle, take me out, then raid her portfolio after the kids are together. They're all in on it, including Joseph. On the call, Patrick kept calling her Jenn, not 'mom,' so this whole story about me being Patrick's father is bullshit."

Eva said, "There's no way he's your son, no resemblance whatsoever. You know, rekindling this has been a bright ray of sunshine. Will we ever have a normal relationship?"

Bill was a little surprised at the twist of the conversation. "When this settles down, we'll have whatever life we want together, I promise. Right now, we need to protect Michelle and eliminate the threats. We need to figure out Espy's involvement, too, to protect her. I'll come up with a plan. When the time comes, you'll be with Michelle, safeguarding her, until I tell you it's over. Leave the rest to me."

Eva, with tears streaming down her face, said, "I can't lose either of my girls. Promise me that won't happen."

Bill looked at Eva. "I promise I'll do everything in my power to protect them."

Eva smiled. "I'm going back inside with Michelle. Goodnight."

Bill smiled, then closed his eyes as Eva left the room.

Chapter 33
Early December 2024

After Eva went back to bed, Bill laid on the couch, unable to get to sleep. With his mind racing over the possibilities, he took out Joseph's phone, scrolling through the pictures again, seeing if he could glean any additional intel. Joseph had lots of pictures, most with young, half-naked girls. The photos of Espy appeared to be at a party, where it looked like she had too much to drink. Her eyes were clearly bloodshot in the photos.

Bill continued through the log, coming across a picture of Uncle Jack, at a family gathering at the Three Aces Pub, not long before he passed. In the photo, there was a group shot of the table. The picture was dated April 4, 2015. Bill noticed in one of the table shots, Jenn was at the table, clear as day. How could she be in witness protection, as well as be at this gathering? Joseph's wife sat next to her, with their arms around each other, looking like they had been long-lost friends. The questions piled up in his head, while Bill was stunned by the betrayal of his family.

It was 5:00 a.m. He mulled this over in his mind, trying to come up with some rationale, but he couldn't, as nothing added up. Why would Joseph have turned on him? Also, why would Uncle Jack accept Jenn at his table, knowing about BJ? After mulling it over, the only conclusion he could come to, was that Jenn needed to be eliminated. Bill went back to the tracking device app and noticed Jenn and Patrick were staying at the same hotel. Joseph was tracking Jenn as well.

Tommy opened the adjacent door. "Figured you were up. Anything new?"

Bill replied, "Went through the photo log. Look at this picture. Notice the date?"

Tommy looked at the photo. "How's that bitch in two places at the same time? Witness protection, my ass!"

Bill responded, "Exactly. Went back to the tracking app. Look at this. They're together."

Tommy asked, "Can that thing tell you the address?"

Bill said, "Pan out a little. They're staying in this hotel!"

Tommy said, "Skipper, you can't make this up. What room are they in?"

Bill replied, "Don't know, we'd need to see the register at the front desk or something from the cleaning staff."

As Tommy and Bill were having this conversation, Eva emerged from the bedroom.

Bill asked, "Michelle still asleep?"

Eva nodded. "Yep. What are you two up to?"

Tommy looked a little sullen while Bill said, "Plotting. Went through the photo log. Found something interesting. Jenn was at Uncle Jack's place in 2015."

Eva said, "Not sure I'm following."

Bill replied, "How could she be in witness protection and at that gathering at the same time? She can't be in two places at once."

Eva looked surprised. "What now?"

Bill replied, "The last thing I noticed was that the tracking software placed them in this hotel."

Eva sternly said, "Can I come with you on this mission?"

Bill shot back, "Absolutely not. You need to protect the girls."

As these words hung in the air, Michelle emerged from the bedroom.

Michelle said, "Dad, when I woke up, I was thinking about something."

Bill said, "What's that, sunshine?"

Michelle replied, "I kept thinking back to how Patrick and I met. I remember the first two times we went out; he was on his phone a lot and kept playing it off as his mom was texting to bother him, but when he put down the phone, I saw he was texting with a man named Joseph. I'm not sure why I remember that now, but I did."

Bill replied, "Sunshine, this whole thing's a setup for them to get to me through you. He's not your brother."

Tommy cut in, "Hey, they're on the move. Seems like they're getting closer. Ambush?"

Bill jumped up, headed into the bedroom, grabbed three XDA 45ACPs, loaded them, and then made sure each weapon had one round in the chamber, as well as the silencers.

Bill walked back into the living room. "Eva, take Michelle to the bathroom. Lay her down in the tub. Here, take this. Eva squat between the tub and the toilet. Proper firing position. Safe word is the same. If you don't hear it, what do you do?"

Eva calmly said, "Empty the weapon into the door, ¾ of the way up."

Bill replied, "Right. Here are two more clips in case you need them. Remember, there are 13 rounds in each clip, plus one in the chamber, count as you shoot. Focus on your breathing. Be comfortable being uncomfortable. This ends right now. This is life and death. I need your help protecting our family."

Eva calmly said, "Michelle, in the bathroom now."

Eva and Michelle went into the bathroom, locking the door behind them. While Eva was squatting down in the bathroom, Tommy went to his room and grabbed his weapon. In 20-second intervals, he called out their attackers' status. As Tommy emerged through the door, Bill said, "Leave that door open. I'll kill the lights. Cover our six from there. I'll get them at the door."

Tommy nodded while Bill turned out the lights, unplugging the lamp and eliminating the switch by the door. They waited close to 5 minutes, with Tommy whispering updates based on Joseph's phone. Bill could hear Michelle sobbing in the tub.

Michelle was crying, "Mom, I'm really scared."

Eva tried to comfort her, "We've got this, man up, Marine. Be comfortable being uncomfortable."

Bill had a slight smile as Eva was taking the credo to heart.

Bill placed his pillow on the couch, covering it with a blanket, giving the appearance that someone was asleep on the couch, a slight diversion, so to speak. Tommy took cover by the adjacent door. Bill was on his left by the desk, close to the front door. Bill heard a click at the front door as if someone had a key to open it.

Seconds later, the door opened. Patrick tried the lights, but nothing happened. Bill waited until both were fully inside.

As the door closed behind them, Jenn whispered, "We've got them. They're asleep."

The door closed behind Jenn. *PUMP, PUMP.* Bill took Patrick out—two shots in the side of his head. When Patrick dropped, Jenn was exposed. *PUMP, PUMP.* Bill put two in the back of Jenn's head. Tommy turned on the lights by the mini bar, while Bill assessed pulses. Neither had one—threats neutralized. Bill felt as if the albatross was lifting from his spirit. In less than one minute, it was over. The girls didn't hear a thing because of the silencers.

Tommy said, "Need to move the girls into the other room. Get out of here quickly."

Bill said, "Why? They attacked us. Self-defense."

Tommy said, "You really want to explain all this to the police?"

Bill replied, "We could tell them we had an altercation at dinner last night. This is how they came at us."

Tommy replied, "Sorry, nobody will believe it."

From behind the door, Bill could hear Eva yelling, "What's happening?"

Bill went up to the door. "OMAHA, it's over."

Eva opened the door, hugging Bill, while Michelle continued to sob in the bathtub.

Eva said, "Thanks for keeping us safe."

Bill responded, "That's my job. Get Michelle out of the tub and into Tommy's room. I'll bring your bag in. We need to get dressed and get out of here quickly. While this was self-defense, it's not in our best interest to tell this story. Look, it's a mess out there, so focus on getting to the door to Tommy's room, nothing else. I'll stand in front of them to obstruct the view."

Tommy then asked, "What do you want to do now?"

Bill said, "They both have weapons in their hands. Let's replace one of the weapons with this one. Do you think we could position one of them to look like one attacked the other?"

Tommy said, "We could, but how did they get into your room after you left?"

Bill replied, "Well, if asked, we can say we got up early to head out. Mention we had an altercation at dinner. We wanted an early start, left the key at the front desk, but nobody was there to collect it. Neither are wearing gloves, so their fingerprints are on the door to prove it, plus they had to have a key to get in. Maybe they came up for revenge, then turned on each other when we weren't here."

Tommy smiled his sly smile. "Skipper, you're one devious marine. I bet you could get OJ off if you were asked."

Bill replied, "Focus so we can get out the door."

At that moment, Eva emerged from the bathroom with Michelle. Bill hadn't been able to provide the obstructed view he promised. What surprised Bill was their reactions. Both looked at the dead bodies with disdain.

Eva said, "Ding dong, the witch's dead."

Michelle said, "Dad, I don't know what to say about the past 24 hours. I thought he was Mr. Right, then he might have been my brother. Now this. How do I ever thank you?"

Bill replied, "Honey, it's my job to protect you. Clearly, I'll go to great lengths to do that. With that said, I need you to get changed so we can leave right away. No showers here. We'll do that in Galveston. Also, when you're done getting changed, give me the clothes you're wearing. I've got a bag here. We'll need to destroy them."

Eva didn't say anything, walking Michelle into the adjacent room. Bill grabbed her bag, bringing it to her. Eva pulled out two outfits, one for each of them. Tommy was in the head, getting changed, so Bill went into his bedroom to change.

It was 05:30 when they left from Tommy's room. When they got downstairs, Bill dropped his one-room key at the front desk, leaving the second upstairs in the room, clearly putting it in Jenn's hand to get her fingerprints on it. Nobody was at the front desk when Bill dropped the key off, but in the distance, he saw the concierge kiosk was occupied.

As they left, the concierge said, "Thank you, come again."

Bill nodded as he headed for the truck. Before leaving the room, Bill instructed Eva and Michelle to exit through the side exit, meeting him and Tommy down the street. There was a Starbucks on the corner that was open 24/7. There weren't a lot of cameras, so splitting up would make it appear like they weren't together, just a coincidence of the time they left the hotel by different exits.

Bill had Michelle and Eva head down a few minutes before Tommy and Bill. Bill told Eva to wait for him at the corner, act like you're leaving, grabbing a coffee, and then he'd get his truck head down the block to pick them at the corner.

As Eva took Michelle out the side entrance, heading for the corner, Tommy and Bill headed out of the lobby to get the truck from the valet. It was 05:45 when Tommy and Bill loaded up on dip getting into the truck. Bill saw Eva and Michelle rounding the corner at the end of the block near 6th Street, standing at the corner. Bill and Tommy got in the truck, then headed up the street and around the corner, stopping to pick up the ladies. Eva and Michelle got in the back seat, and Michelle immediately put her head in Eva's lap, softly sobbing.

Before Michelle fell asleep, she said, "Dad. I love you so much."

Bill said, "Love you too! Get some sleep."

Michelle asked, "Dad when we get home, can you please tell us the story? I'll admit, waiting this long has scared me, but after the last 24 hours, maybe I better understand your perspective."

Bill replied, "Let's get home first."

Tommy texted Amanda, "We're heading out now, be home before lunch. Can't wait to see you."

Michelle closed her eyes, nestling into Eva's lap. Soon, they were over the 6th Street bridge. Three and a half hours before they're home.

Chapter 34
Early December 2024

The ride to Galveston was quiet, especially that early in the morning. They didn't stop on the ride home either, as everyone was worn out from the last couple of days. Bill dropped Tommy off first, and Amanda greeted them in the driveway. As they got out, Amanda noticed their tired faces but also sensed relief, though she wasn't exactly sure what had happened.

Amanda walked over. "Michelle, Eva, it's so nice to see you. I've got coffee on if you'd like to stay for a bit."

Eva said, "A coffee would be terrific."

Michelle asked, "Aunt Amanda, do you have any raspberry tarts? Mom, these tarts are the bomb."

Amanda smiled. "I knew you were coming, so I made some just for you. Took them out of the oven 30 minutes ago. Go help yourself."

Michelle ran up the stairs, calling out, "They're all mine!"

The adults chuckled as they made their way upstairs. Bill, knowing how good those tarts were, figured Michelle would surrender at least one to her dad.

When they reached the top of the stairs, the breeze felt amazing, and the sun was warm on their faces. Eva and Amanda hit it off this time, sharing old stories about their two marine warhorses. Tommy and Bill sat back, enjoying their coffee and basking in the glow of their ladies.

Bill asked Tommy, "When did you want to take care of the package?"

Tommy replied, "Let's get it done now!"

Amanda asked, "So, whatever happened to Jenn and this kid, Patrick?"

Eva almost spit out the sip of coffee she had in her mouth.

Tommy looked at Amanda. "We'll have no more trouble from the likes of them."

Amanda smiled at Bill, sensing his satisfaction in finally putting down the threats and laying to rest some of his past. With just a smile, Amanda could say so much.

After that awkward moment, they all sat together, talking for two hours before Eva, Michelle, and Bill went back to Bill's house.

As they were leaving, Amanda asked, "Would you like to come for supper? I've got some nice chicken cutlets."

Bill looked at Eva as if asking for her permission.

Eva said, "Wonderful. Do you want us to bring anything?"

Amanda replied, "Bring some wine, maybe dessert. Nothing fancy."

Eva smiled. "What time?"

Bill answered, "18:00 is always supper time here."

Amanda smiled. "A well-trained marine."

Eva laughed out loud. "See you at 18:00."

They left, making their way to Bill's house. Bill left Tommy by the smoldering fire; the clothes now destroyed. As they pulled into

Bill's driveway, a Texas State Trooper's car was parked on the street outside Bill's house.

Eva asked, "What's this?"

Bill replied, "Don't know. Whatever I say, swear to it."

They got out of the truck as Bill pulled the luggage from the truck bed, pretending not to give the trooper much notice. At that moment, the trooper stepped out of his car.

The trooper said, "Excuse me, Bill Quinn?"

Bill replied, "Yes. What can I do for you, Trooper?"

The trooper said, "I've got a few questions for you if you've got a minute."

Bill asked, "Is it okay if the ladies head upstairs? We were on the road early this morning."

The trooper replied, "Sure."

Eva and Michelle took their cue and headed upstairs.

Bill responded, "Thanks. What can I help you with?"

The trooper asked, "Can you account for your whereabouts over the past 24 hours?"

Bill said, "Sure. Drove to Nashville to visit an old friend the day before. She's the older woman who just went upstairs. We had dinner and spent the evening together before heading out early to go to Austin yesterday. It's a bit of a long story, we were involved 20 years ago, which resulted in the younger girl who also went upstairs. She's my daughter."

The trooper said, "And where else have you been over the past 24 hours?"

Bill continued, "We thought we'd surprise our daughter. We're rekindling our relationship after many years. So, from Nashville, we drove to Austin. My daughter goes to school at UT. We surprised her, told her about us getting back together, and then took her out to dinner."

The trooper asked, "What about last night at dinner?"

Bill replied, "Met Michelle for dinner. She brought her new boyfriend and his mother. As it turned out, the mother was my ex-wife from 35 years ago. Suffice it to say, things didn't go well, and the table broke up very quickly—even before dinner was served. I felt the kid's mother made a bit of a scene out of it. I'm sure our waiter heard all of it. I recall him commenting after the mother and boy left the table. He came over to tell us he was holding our dinners and that the conversation at the table looked heated. He wasn't wrong."

The trooper shot back, "And what happened after dinner?"

Bill replied, "We went upstairs, had an early night. Got up early, as I wanted to be home before noon. I think we were out the door by 05:30. We stopped by a friend's place when we got back—went for coffee. We were there maybe two hours before pulling up here."

The trooper asked, "Anything else happen?"

Bill calmly replied, "Not that I recall. Why are you curious about my whereabouts?"

The trooper said, "What time did you check out this morning?"

Bill replied, "Early. It was before 5:30 if memory serves. I wanted to be on the road to beat any traffic. When we left the hotel, nobody was at the front desk, so I left the *key* on the desk where someone would find them. I thought it was strange nobody was manning the desk, but I do remember a young man at the concierge desk. I'm pretty sure he had brown hair, maybe 6'2"."

The trooper stated, "Mr. Quinn, the room you stayed in last night—a man and a woman were found dead on the living room floor. One of them had your number in their contact list. The woman's name was Maura Jennifer McTiernay. Do you know her?"

Bill replied, "I was married to her a long time ago, like I said earlier. Haven't had much contact with her over the years—maybe once or twice in the past 12 months, with a 20+-year gap before that. She told me she'd come out of witness protection at the time after her father died. I've got no idea if that's true. We lost touch after she moved out, not long after our son died."

The trooper replied, "Thanks for confirming she was your ex-wife. She was found with a young man, say 20 to 25. Know anything about him?"

Bill said, "Can't be sure. Like I said, she told me she never remarried or had more children, so I'm not sure who this young man is."

The trooper, trying to gauge his reaction, said, "Did you see her in the restaurant last night?"

Bill responded, "As I said before, we did. We were having dinner when Jenn showed up at the table unexpectedly with this young man, playing it off like it was a pure coincidence. They sat down at our table, uninvited. She said she came to tell me this young man was her son and that I was his father. Suffice to say, I was shocked."

"Long before my son died, our relationship was a train wreck, so we hadn't been together for well over a year. Eva—the older woman who went upstairs—said she saw nothing to indicate this young man was my son. After some heated exchanges, I demanded a DNA test to confirm. At that point, they got up from the table and left the restaurant. It was an ugly night, to say the least."

The trooper said, "Interesting she came out of the shadows after all this time."

Bill replied, "All I'll say is, she's like a bad penny always turns up when you least expect it, leaves chaos in her wake too. I hate to speak ill of her, but that's been my experience with her. Not sure what else to say."

Bill was trying to defuse the conversation. The trooper took down his notes, seeming to piece together what had happened.

The trooper asked, "Can I show you a picture of the deceased?"

Bill said, "Sure."

The trooper pulled up his phone and showed Bill the picture, watching his reaction closely. Bill maintained a solemn indifference, acknowledging the gravity of two people being dead but offering nothing further. This wasn't the first time he'd seen a dead body.

The trooper finally asked, "Is this Maura McTiernay?"

Bill replied, "It looks like her. Is that a room key next to her on the floor?"

The trooper looked surprised. "Interesting observation. We didn't notice that. Perhaps she took the key, but why the room you stayed in last night?"

Bill replied, "Honestly, I haven't got a clue."

Eva appeared on the balcony. "Is everything okay?"

Bill looked up, nodding yes but saying nothing.

He then asked the trooper, "Do you need to speak with them?"

The trooper replied, "No, I got what I came for. Thanks for pointing out the room key. I'll let you go. Thanks for your assistance."

Bill nodded affirmatively, then walked to the back of the truck, fiddling around in the back seat as he waited for the trooper to leave. Within a minute, the trooper sped off.

When the trooper was out of sight, Bill removed the luggage from the bed of his truck. The smartest thing he'd done was leave the burn bag at Tommy's house, including Joseph's phone. Tommy had burned the bag before Bill left. Bill was sure Tommy would tell Amanda what had happened.

When Bill got to the top of the stairs, Eva was waiting near the door. As he opened it, Eva leapt at him, giving him a huge hug.

Bill asked, "What's this?"

Eva said, "I really thought he was taking you away."

Michelle came into the living room and sat on the couch. "Dad, everything okay?"

Bill replied, "Yes. Let's head to the beach. We could use some sun."

Eva responded, "Sounds perfect."

Michelle said, "I'll get my sweater. Mom and I will fix a snack bag."

Bill smiled. "Great. I'll get the chairs together."

He grabbed his sunglasses before heading downstairs to the garage to retrieve the chairs. After retrieving the chairs, Eva and Michelle came down the stairs, each carrying a blanket to cover their legs while sitting on the beach.

Eva looked at Bill. "You need some sunscreen on your neck."

Bill replied, "Sure."

After Eva applied sunscreen to his neck, they all headed to the beach. Once they got situated, Michelle sat reading a book while Eva and Bill strolled down to the water. Eva dipped her bare feet into the waves.

"Wow, that's warmer than I thought," Eva said.

Bill replied, "It's always warmer in the bay. It's shallow."

Eva smiled. "It's wonderful. You know, it feels like we've got everything in front of us now."

Bill didn't reply immediately. He gazed out over the horizon, the calmness settling over him.

Finally, he asked, "What about Espy?"

Eva said, "I need to talk to her, but I don't want her to find out about what's happened. I love her, but she can't keep a secret. Your daughter over there, though—she'll keep her mouth shut. When are you telling her the story?"

Bill said, "Soon."

Eva replied, "Bill, you've been saying that for a month. After last night, she needs to know. When you were downstairs getting the chairs, she said to me, *can you believe how badass Dad is? I knew he was overprotective, but he's on a whole other level.*"

Bill shook his head. "She doesn't get it."

Eva said, "She understands more than you think. You've said it yourself; she's not stupid. In many ways, she gets the best parts of her from you."

Bill laughed. "She's all you. Beautiful, tough, stubborn, and passionate about the people who matter most to her."

Eva smiled. "Honey, you just described yourself."

Bill now realized that no matter what he said, he'd already lost this argument. Better to let it go. For Bill, that was growth. In the past, he would've dug in deeper and fought harder, but this time, he let it rest.

Eva and Bill headed back to the chairs, sitting quietly, reading, enjoying the sun, and the breeze off the water. Bill's thoughts wandered to how Eva was going to handle the situation with Espy. His gut told him it was likely just a party-girl phase Espy had gotten tangled up in. While those thoughts lingered, Eva's phone rang.

Eva answered, "Hey, Espy, how's it going?"

Bill and Michelle could hear Eva's side of the conversation, though it wasn't much, as Espy seemed to be talking at lightning speed from the look on Eva's face.

Eva said, "Interesting. The police stopped by to question you?"

A few minutes passed. Then Eva said, "You had your picture taken where?"

After another pause, Eva exclaimed, "Are you kidding me? You went to his hotel? Why?"

Within seconds, Eva's voice rose. "So, what you're telling me is, you went to a party I didn't know about at a hotel downtown, hooked up with some loser you didn't know, and then thought it was a good idea to let him take *lewd* photos? What were you thinking?"

Another minute went by, with Michelle and Bill exchanging intrigued glances.

Eva said, "He's dead?"

After a brief silence, Eva added, "You say his name was Joseph? He called you the other night but hung up after you answered. I'm glad you told me the truth. I'm not happy about this, but we'll deal with it when I'm home."

Before ending the call, Eva said, "Yes, the trip to Galveston was uneventful."

That last comment prompted chuckles from Bill and Michelle. Eva then ended the call and looked at Bill. "Espy was questioned by the police."

Bill nodded. "Figured as much. Based on those photos."

Michelle raised an eyebrow, her expression clearly asking, *What photos?*

Eva continued, "One of the managers at the hotel remembered her from a party where she met Joseph and partied with him most of the night. He recalled her because he had to respond to a noise complaint around 1:00 a.m. due to loud music and dancing coming from Joseph's room."

Michelle asked, "Espy was partying with a stranger at a hotel?"

Eva replied, "She met him through a friend—the same girl involved in that bad drug deal in Nashville, also probably her new lover boy. She said the police were following up on potential leads. Nothing more."

Bill, unsure of what to say, stood up from his chair and started walking toward the water's edge.

As he walked away, he said, "Glad it's over. I'm heading to the shoreline."

Michelle said, "Dad, can I come?"

Bill said, "Sure."

It was clear Eva needed a moment to process everything Espy had shared. When Michelle and Bill reached the water, he noticed Michelle glancing back to make sure Eva was out of earshot. Once Michelle felt confident they wouldn't be overheard, she spoke.

"Dad, I've got something to tell you. That's not the first time Espy's done something like that. She's been doing reckless stuff like that ever since Angel died."

Bill replied, "Really? That's a shame. Does your mom know about any of it?"

Michelle hesitated before answering. "Dad, the guy Espy's dating is a dirtbag—the biggest drug dealer in our high school."

Bill asked, "Does your mom know? Maybe she should."

Michelle sighed. "Espy's been out of control, but this is the first time the police have been involved. Mom suspects she's got a problem. She's tried talking to her several times, but Espy's not ready to deal with it. It's got me worried, especially with some of her posts on *X*. Mom would lose her shit if she saw them."

Bill said, "That's a shame. Espy needs to be ready to deal with her problems on her own timetable. I appreciate you're worried about her, but she must want to help herself. In the meantime, you need to focus on you. This is your time to be a little selfish, so to speak."

Michelle changed the subject. "You and Mom, huh?"

Bill replied, "Honey, I don't know what's going to happen. We're trying to put the baggage away and see if we can work it out."

Michelle smiled softly. "I get it. Just be honest with her. That's all I ask. Dad, isn't that Natalie?"

Bill turned to look, sure enough, Natalie was walking straight toward them.

When Natalie reached them, she said coldly, "Bill."

She didn't bother acknowledging Michelle.

Bill replied, "Been a while. What can I do for you?"

Natalie glanced at Michelle. "Can you excuse us? This won't take long."

Michelle hesitated, looking nervous, then nodded, walking back toward the chairs to sit with Eva.

Once Michelle was out of earshot, Bill asked, "Natalie, what can I do for you?"

Natalie said, "I can't be in a relationship with you. It's too complicated. There are too many distractions, making it quite impossible. Too many lies. The return from Austin made that all quite clear."

Bill replied, "Okay. Anything else?"

Natalie shouted, "That's all you've got to say?"

Bill stated calmly. "First of all, you were just rude to Michelle— not even saying hello to her— then dismissed her like she was a speck of shit on your shoe. It's fine if you wanted a private chat, but treating her disrespectfully? It's not okay."

"Second, I've reached out numerous times trying to engage, and you gave me nothing. Now you show up with some story about how complicated my life is. You know what? I'm glad to see your true colors."

Natalie's face twisted in anger. She slapped him hard on his right cheek and shouted, "Fuck you!"

Bill smiled. "Not anymore. It was very nice to see you again. Good luck and goodbye."

Natalie turned and stormed away. As she left, Bill gazed out over the horizon into Galveston Bay for at least ten minutes. It was the most peaceful moment he'd experienced in a long while. For the first time, he felt things were falling into place in a good way. Yet, a lingering fear crept in—how long would it stay this way? Bill never trusted happiness. Only time could tell.

After a while, he returned to his chair.

Michelle looked at him. "Dad, you okay?"

Bill smirked. "I'm fine. It's not like I didn't see it coming when we spotted her."

Michelle responded, "For what it's worth, Natalie was a strange lady. Amy told me she can be sweet but vicious. I saw it with Amy once or twice."

Bill said, "I'm not sure what to say to that other than that's someone else's problem now."

Michelle replied, "Dad, we've been here for a couple of hours. When are we going to hear this story?"

Bill smiled. "Let's head up and shower. If we don't dilly-dally, I can probably tell it before dinner. Or would you rather wait until after dinner, back at the house, with some cocktails and a fire?"

Michelle replied instantly, "How about now? I'm tired of waiting!"

Bill glanced at Eva, who gave him a look that said, *She's your daughter.* He looked around, noticing that no one else was in earshot.

Bill sighed. "Okay. You want a bedtime story that'll set your hair on fire? Here goes. Eva, you've heard most of this story, but there are parts I may have missed. I'm not sure if I left anything out. But when I'm done, this box is closed forever."

Eva replied sternly, "Go on!"

Bill began the story by starting with Belfast, his USMC deployment, and then Fatima. As Bill recounted the events, Michelle was swept up in the romantic tale of his evening spent with Fatima. Eva, however, wasn't as enchanted. She sat quietly, her expression revealing that part of the story stung.

Bill described the firefight and what he believed had happened to Fatima.

Michelle asked, "You never found her?"

Bill replied, "No, honey. I didn't know what had happened to her until a friend found her in Kuwait several years later. It was the first time I didn't protect someone I loved. I swore it would never happen again."

Bill noticed that Eva was growing visibly uncomfortable with the conversation.

He paused. "Eva, I'm not trying to hurt you with this. You wanted the whole story."

Eva nodded but remained silent, so Bill continued. He told about his Royal friend that he rescued, about the Colonel and Martinez, the numerous weapons cache seizures, the Spanish-speaking personnel loading the trucks, and his meeting with the Queen and the Royal Family.

Each detail painted a vivid picture, but it was clear that the weight of the past lingered heavily over the present.

Michelle said, "So you met the Queen of England?"

Bill replied, "Yes, my unit helped rescue the future King."

Eva said, "That must have been cool."

Bill nodded. "It was."

He then transitioned into how he met Jenn and the events that unfolded in Boston.

Michelle asked, "Did you ever find out who those men were?"

Bill replied, "No. Uncle Jack thought they were with Owen, but we never knew for sure."

As Bill told the story, he watched their reactions. More than once, both Michelle and Eva covered their mouths with their hands, visibly shocked. Bill thought Eva was doing it for affect, having heard the story the day before. Still, they stayed focused, intent on letting Bill finish the story. Even they could sense how painful it was for him to relive those moments.

Bill continued, recounting what happened after Boston—how things with Jenn were resolved and how he started his life with her, for her. He talked about her pregnancy and the four years after BJ was born.

Then he told them about BJ's kidnapping and death. When he revealed Owen had killed BJ, both Eva and Michelle were in tears. They listened as Bill described the days following the funeral—the confrontation with Owen, the involvement of Uncle Jack, the Colonel, and Martinez. He then spoke of Eva's blunder at the funeral.

He detailed the waterfront drop-off with Owen, the brutal beating he gave him before dropping him off, and how he'd returned home afterward, finding a way to move on one day at a time.

Bill then transitioned to how he met Eva and how things started between them.

Michelle asked, "You were both married when this happened?"

Bill said, "Yes. Both of us were in very unhappy marriages. At first, we connected because of that—or at least that's how I see it."

Eva agreed. "That's right. Things with Angel were bad when I met Bill."

Bill moved on to their breakup, admitting he had always wondered if Michelle was his daughter.

Michelle asked, "Why didn't you ask for a DNA test then?"

Eva replied, "How could we? I was trying to keep the affair a secret. I didn't succeed, as he knew about the affair from the Colonel."

Eva was clearly growing tense, but Bill decided to continue the story. He talked about meeting the Colonel at the gym and at Uncle

Jack's funeral. He recounted what Martinez said about Eva at the funeral.

Eva blurted out, "He was a pig!"

Michelle smirked at Eva's reaction, but Bill kept going. He spoke about moving to Galveston and the peace that came with it—until Eva called 17 years later.

Finally, he described what it felt like to know Michelle was his daughter. When he finished with that part of the story, both Eva and Michelle were in tears again.

Bill transitioned into what happened on the way back from Austin with Michelle, delving into the Seamus affair. Eva only knew the broad strokes of that story, so Bill filled in the details. Talking about Joseph was difficult. As kids, they'd been close, and it pained Bill to think Uncle Jack might have wanted him dead. He would never know for sure if Joseph was spinning a lie for his own advantage.

Bill described what happened in Room 705—finding the young girl convulsing in the bedroom and his tense exchange with Joseph. Neither Eva nor Michelle seemed particularly phased by those details. Their reactions almost conveyed a sense of *yeah, that makes sense.*

Michelle asked, "So all of this was to protect us? It started because you couldn't protect Fatima. Dad, it's not your fault what happened to Fatima."

Eva shifted uncomfortably, and Bill noticed immediately.

He turned to her. "Are you okay with this? You seem very uncomfortable."

Eva stood up, tears forming in her eyes. "I know I asked for it, but it's hard to listen to. It's hard to know you loved Fatima and never told me. Why wouldn't you tell me, even back in our original Nashville days?"

Bill sighed. "It was too painful to talk about Fatima. Do you know Tommy and I have never spoken about her after that day? Tommy was with me when it happened. Even after I knew she was alive, I couldn't talk about it with him, only mentioning it to him when you last visited, how could I ever explain it to you?"

Eva was crying now. "Did you tell Jenn about Fatima? What about Natalie?"

Bill shook his head. "No, you're the only one who's ever known about Fatima. I never talked to Jenn or Natalie about her."

"You know what? Maybe Tommy's right. I should've just laid this down and never told it. Look at the unnecessary pain it's causing. I must've been out of my mind."

Michelle looked upset, perhaps at how Bill expressed himself, but she didn't say anything. Instead, she turned toward the shoreline, watching the waves roll in. Michelle seemed to have a better grasp of the situation than Eva. While Bill approached his emotions with logic, Eva was a live wire—every thought, positive or negative, intertwined while sparking emotion.

Bill could see Eva was livid. She kept removing her sunglasses to wipe away tears, clearly wanting to explode. Yet every time she opened her mouth, no words came out.

After a few minutes of awkward silence, Eva finally asked, "Are you done?"

Bill replied, "Yes. Clearly, I don't need to go into last night."

Michelle broke the tension. "Dad, thanks for telling the story. It's a lot to take in. But as I listened, all I kept thinking about was something you've always said: *It's your job to protect us. When they come at you, they always come at what you love.*"

Bill nodded. "That's true. My biggest failures were not protecting Fatima, BJ, even your mom. I tried but failed in those moments. I've got to live with that. I think that's why I'm so protective of you."

Eva, her voice calmer now but still carrying an edge, asked, "What about me in that equation?"

Bill turned to her. "The same goes for you, no matter what happens between us. You're an extension of Michelle. I've been in a toxic marriage before, but we're restarting this—fresh, with no more secrets, right?"

Eva hesitated, then smiled softly. "Sorry, it felt like I was on the outside looking in. Agreed, no more secrets. So, you're done? Time to pack the box, put them away—or maybe even destroy them?"

Bill exhaled deeply. "Yes. I'm tired of carrying this boulder with me. Also, last call for questions. Once these boxes are closed, they're closed for good."

Michelle, after a moment asked, "Hypothetically, if you found Fatima, how do you think things would've been different?"

Bill said, "That's a question that prompts too much speculation. Life is always full of possibilities, fulfillments, and regrets. You don't get many do-overs in life. Hopefully, we learn from our past and the lessons it teaches us."

Eva blurted out, "So, it's time to put the boxes away. I've got no more questions. I'm not sure I can handle much more."

She stood up and walked to the water's edge alone. A minute later, Michelle got up to follow her and console her mother. Bill wasn't upset by Eva's reaction; it was natural after hearing all of this. He knew enough about Eva to recognize when she was pushed too far, she shuts down, needing time to process it in her own way.

Bill sat quietly, staring out over the water, trying to push the story out of his mind and find some serenity. But he still felt no relief. It wasn't cathartic. There was no emotional release. It felt like nothing more than a relaxing day in the sun while pushing the boulder further.

By 4:00 p.m., Bill realized he was parched after recounting the tale.

Heading toward the water, he called out to the ladies, "I'm heading up for a drink. Want anything?"

Michelle said, "A bottle of water."

Eva smirked. "Four fingers with a large rock."

Bill laughed. "I can make that happen."

With that, he headed back to the house to grab the drinks.

As he approached the house, he saw someone standing on the front steps. A pit formed in his stomach as he muttered to himself, *What now?*

When he reached the base of the driveway, his fears subsided—it was the Amazon delivery lady making her way down the steps after dropping off a package.

Bill smiled. "Hello. Thanks."

The Amazon lady smiled back as she crossed the driveway and into her truck.

Bill thought—*finally, no drama at the base of his stairs.*

PS Cleary

PS Cleary is a first-time author who has explored a family's story over three books in his series. Had it not been for his desire to take some time away from his career, who knows if he would ever have endeavored in such a project?

Cleary has served in numerous Executive Leadership roles in the financial services sector spanning over 30 years. He has been married to his wife, Cheryl, for 30+ years, building a life of mutual respect and love. Together they have two adult children, one an aspiring chef and a second who is afflicted with Autism. They are strong advocates for special needs causes, active in their local communities.

He likes to play golf and re-finish furniture. In addition, he is an avid hockey and Red Sox fan.